"I am the count," he said.

She smiled. "Vlad Dracul. Yes, I can see that. Your costume is wonderful. I meant, who are you really?"

His smile deepened. "The count, *mademoiselle*. I am Jon Vadim, the count."

He kept his eyes on her. Carly wanted to tear her gaze from his, but could not.

He touched her chin, caressing it lightly. "Welcome to Westphalen, Carly Kiernan."

She felt his touch, and her flesh grew hot. So this was Count Vadim. She had been warned about him....

His smile suddenly seemed cold. "All right. Fantasy time is over, Ms. Kiernan. Now tell me, who are you really, and what do you want here?"

Dear Reader,

When two people fall in love, the world is suddenly new and exciting, and it's that same excitement we bring to you in Silhouette Intimate Moments. These are stories with scope, with grandeur. The characters lead the lives we all dream of, and everything they do reflects the wonder of being in love.

Longer and more sensuous than most romances, Silhouette Intimate Moments novels take you away from everyday life and let you share the magic of love. Adventure, glamour, drama, even suspense— these are the passwords that let you into a world where love has a power beyond the ordinary, where the best authors in the field today create stories of love and commitment that will stay with you always.

In coming months look for novels by your favorite authors: Maura Seger, Parris Afton Bonds, Linda Howard and Nora Roberts, to name just a few. And whenever you buy books, look for all the Silhouette Intimate Moments, love stories *for* today's women *by* today's women.

Leslie J. Wainger
Senior Editor
Silhouette Books

Heather Graham Pozzessere
This Rough Magic

Silhouette Intimate Moments

Published by Silhouette Books New York

America's Publisher of Contemporary Romance

SILHOUETTE BOOKS
300 East 42nd St., New York, N.Y. 10017

ISBN: 0-373-07260-0

First Silhouette Books printing October 1988

HEATHER GRAHAM POZZESSERE

considers herself lucky to live in Florida, where she can indulge her love of water sports, like swimming and boating, year-round. Her background includes stints as a model, an actress and a bartender. She was once actually tied to the railroad tracks to garner publicity for the dinner theater where she was acting. Now she's a full-time wife, mother of four and, of course, a writer of historical and contemporary romances.

This book is dedicated with
lots of love and all the very best to
my cousin
Dennis Staples
and to his brother, David,
and to his parents,
Eddy and Eileen...
but only if they behave!

Chapter 1

The moon rose high over the misty night, bright, round and full. It cast an eerie glow upon the shrouded forests that sat on either side of the ancient trail that led to Castle Vadim.

A wolf howled. It was a lonely, haunting sound in the darkness. Despite herself, Carly Kiernan felt a rivulet of chills cascade down her spine. In her corner of the elegant Vadim carriage, she smiled to herself, holding back the velvet drapery at the small window to see the peculiar beauty of the night. The count, it seemed, was being granted some magnificent special effects for his Halloween party.

But then, what else? Castle Vadim sat high upon the picturesque Carpathian mountains, in the Duchy of Westphalen, which bordered Romania. Like Transylvania, its other neighbor, Westphalen was a land of legend, of baying dogs and howling wolves, of the real Vlad Dracul, the Impaler. By day the castle was a splendid Gothic structure, her sister, Jasmine, had assured Carly. It was impeccably clean and elegant. No cobweb would dare to dust its ancient rock.

But by night, as Carly could see now, the castle stood implacable and chilling, surrounded by a surreal, yellowish glow, turrets and towers rising stark against the moonlit sky.

The wolf howled again. Plaintively.

Despite herself, Carly shivered once more. This was a far cry from Manhattan, where the mass of buildings created a landscape of pure concrete, where neon and glitter, noise and bustle were the order of the day.

Carly was struck by the sheer loneliness of this place. Miles of forest and swirling mist separated each tiny village from the next, and the shrouding fog seemed to rule eternally, resting upon the ground, dancing within the trees, creating imagery, fantasy and the magic of illusion.

And that wolf! She could hear the creature's cry over the sounds of the hooves of the black stallions that pulled the eighteenth-century carriage, over the grating of the wheels and the jolting of the coach body. The cry hung on the night air, and each time she heard it, she shivered with some primal fear. This was the modern world, and she knew she was perfectly safe. Wolves did prowl the woods, but she would soon be at the castle—safe from the beasts of the night, if nothing else.

She frowned, leaning back, watching the moon with its ivory circle of haze. The atmosphere was fascinating, marvelous. She couldn't believe that she was here, and she wouldn't have been here if it hadn't been for Jasmine.

Carly opened her evening bag and fingered the letter that had come to her in the States last week. She smoothed out the paper and read the words again.

Carly, I know that you have been hesitating, but you must come here for the Halloween party! The count is wonderful. I'm so very excited. I need you. I really need you. You must come!

Jasmine ran a travel agency that was very popular with the jet set, and she was always jaunting off somewhere. Carly had known about the party—she had planned costumes for herself and her sister months ago—though she hadn't decided whether to really come or not until she received the letter. But the words "I need you. I really need you" had bothered Carly.

Carly was even more disturbed now, because she hadn't been able to contact Jasmine since she arrived this afternoon. Her calls to the castle had been answered by a confused maid. It seemed as if the count didn't want to see her or even talk to her. Actually, it seemed as if he wanted her to go home. Carly had even tried to explain about Jasmine, and that she'd been invited herself.

At long last the concierge at her hotel had appeared at her door to tell her that the count would see her at the party and would send his coach for her at eight.

Jasmine had so forcibly tried to persuade her to come, and now this count, whom Jasmine was so crazy about, was behaving incredibly rudely.

Staring out at the night sky as they lurched along, Carly remembered how it had all begun. Jasmine had come to see her in New York between trips, and she had already been talking about Count Vadim's costume ball. Carly designed costumes for a living, and Jasmine was convinced that she could help Carly's career through her acquaintances.

"The ball will be wonderful for you professionally," Jasmine had assured her. "You must wear the blue silk Empire gown with the velvet cloak. It's the most stunning outfit I've ever seen. Geoffrey Taylor will be there, and I'm sure he'll demand you do the work for his next play." She had added softly, "And you'll have to come out of that cocoon you've spun around yourself since Tim. It'll be good for you."

Carly had been hesitant, and it now appeared that Jasmine had known it. But Carly had thought even then about coming.

It was more than the professional benefit. She had felt that she needed to come. She had been hiding for a long time, and maybe she was ready to meet the world again. Or maybe she wasn't really ready to meet the world at all, but the tiny duchy was so different that there she could more easily reenter society. Perhaps she did not have to come into the world as herself at all; her entire time here could be a wonderful dress-up party, and she could pretend that she was living a dream.

"You'll like Geoffrey," Jasmine had assured her. It didn't really matter to Carly whether she liked the man or not; she wanted only a professional association with him. He produced the kind of plays she found fascinating, wonderful extravaganzas, and she longed to design the costumes for just one of his plays.

"Ah...and just wait until you meet the count!" Jasmine had teased her with wide eyes.

"Count Dracula?"

"You laugh, my dear child," Jasmine warned, shaking a finger at her. "I'm talking about Count Vadim, of course, but I warn you, my sweet innocent, his effect is the same.''

"Is it?" Carly had been amused. She and Jasmine were very different women. Jasmine was a whirl of emotion; Carly was more careful. It often seemed to her that a part had died with Tim, that she could not feel again.

"Just wait," Jasmine warned her sagely. "I've seen many a supersavvy jet-setter lose her heart, virtue—and her very soul—over the man."

"Her very soul?"

"Be a smarty," Jasmine retorted. "You'll see!"

Just what was going on? Carly wondered. She hadn't been able to see much of her sister lately, and in fact, Jasmine had been in a big hurry in New York. She had simply taken her altered harem costume and left.

Forgetting the conversation with her sister, Carly suddenly sat up, her frown deepening. The coachman seemed to be going faster and faster, and from inside the ancient carriage, Carly thought his speed didn't seem at all safe.

"Hey!" she protested as a sudden jolt sent her crashing against the side of the carriage. She didn't know if "Hey!" translated as anything into French, the official language of the duchy. It wouldn't matter; he would never hear her over the clatter of the hooves.

She steadied herself, biting her lower lip in perplexity. She wasn't entirely sure what she was doing in the carriage, anyway. She would have gladly called a cab. But the concierge at the hotel had assured her that the carriage was very real, that it had been in the Vadim family for generations. With its velvet seats and carved coat of arms, massive wheels and elegant brass folding steps, it was beautiful. The stallions wore plumes on their bridles, and Carly thought the whole thing resembled Cinderella's fabulous carriage.

She wasn't at all thrilled with her curious transportation at the moment. They were going far too fast, and she wished she'd been picked up in the Vadim Lamborghini. Carly didn't know a great deal about the roads here nor about eighteenth-century carriages, but she did know that the speed of this one couldn't possibly agree with the condition of the road.

Carly clutched at the ancient velvet seats to steady herself.

"Hey! Stop! Slow down!" she called out. She gritted her teeth, wondering if the driver was insane, wondering if she was about to be pitched into the valley far, far below.

"Please!" she cried. She tried to reach the window, but the tremendous pitching and swaying of the carriage sent her sliding back.

Hadn't there been a movie like this? she wondered uneasily. A dark night with a full moon, a misted forest and the cry of a wolf. A carriage wrecked within the fog-shrouded forest, and a woman left there alone, vulnerable, frightened, easy prey?...

For the terrors of the night.

A full moon. The time for demons, for witchcraft and satanism...and werewolves. And here she was, on All Hallows' Eve, in the mountainous region so very near Transylvania....

Don't be absurd! Carly raged to herself in silence. She didn't need to be afraid of a legend. What she needed was to be wary of the very real danger that threatened her now, the runaway carriage. Her life was in peril; the vehicle could overturn at any moment.

"Please! Driver! Sir!"

Against the jolting, she managed to pull herself to the window and held on with all her strength. The carriage veered, but she wound her fingers around the wooden frame and brought her head just outside the window so that she could look for the driver.

"Sir!"

The moon passed behind a sudden cloud, then came out again. Cold panic seized Carly.

There was no driver. The coachman's seat loomed dark and empty beneath the glow of the moonlight.

"No!" she whispered.

Her grip upon the frame went limp. The carriage slammed and jolted, and she went flying to the opposite side. Her head struck the paneling—hard.

For a moment she saw stars. Her head cleared and she tried to sit up again; she needed desperately to think. She'd surely kill herself if she jumped.

Yet if she remained inside as the horses careened along at this gallop, she would surely be cast over the side of the mountain when they came around one of the perilous curves.

Suddenly, the carriage veered, slowed somewhat, then lost a wheel. Carly screamed as the carriage slammed down with a horrible rending sound. She prayed almost mindlessly, certain that her life was at an end.

Then the carriage spun and tumbled. Carly screamed again as she was thrown savagely about. Her head banged against the roof of the vehicle, and blackness followed.

Carly opened her eyes slowly. She had no idea how long she'd been out. She blinked, thinking that she had a hell of a headache. She looked above her, and the moon was still shining.

Painfully, she raised herself on her elbows.

She was still in the carriage, or what was left of it. The vehicle's frame had broken apart. She lay upon a velvet seat, but that seat lay on the ground.

It was as if a sudden twister had picked up the carriage and tossed it to the ground in a frenzy.

Carly groaned aloud, pressing on her temples. She flexed her fingers and her toes, then her arms and legs. She was all right, she decided with relief. She was disheveled and disoriented but otherwise alive and well.

Just as she was congratulating herself on her well-being, the wolf howled again.

The sound was so much louder now. Frightening.

The wolf was near. Trying to stagger to her feet among the wreckage, Carly looked around. She was in a small clearing. Thank God the carriage had crashed into the forest, she thought, and not over the edge of the rugged mountain road.

But the mist was heavy around her. It swirled against her, covered the base of the trees and made an eerie enigma of the forest.

The wolf could be anywhere. He could be watching her from the cover of the trees.

There was a sudden rustling to her left. Carly tried to spin around. She cried out, aware suddenly that her ankle was injured. In pain she fell back against the seat, straining to see through the mist.

Something was out there. The rustling came again, and her heart began to pound.

A cloud hid the moon once more. Total darkness descended upon her.

Her breathing was ragged and desperate as she blinked into the total darkness. "Oh, God!" she whispered.

Then she assured herself that she didn't believe in ghosts or goblins, werewolves or vampires or anything that went bump in the night.

No...she didn't believe in ghosts or in mythical beings.

But she was in the Carpathian mountains. And a full moon was hidden by a black cloud and she was alone and hurt on a mist-shrouded mountain where wolves preyed....

"Don't be silly," she warned herself aloud, needing to hear the sound of her own voice. She didn't usually have a wild imagination, and wasn't easily frightened. She was a New Yorker. She lived in a city with any number of wolves and bloodsuckers; it was just that those wolves and tricksters walked upright and spoke with smooth voices. In the city, she carried her Mace.

But in these mountains...

She could imagine an old gypsy woman warning Lon Chaney, Jr. that the curse of the werewolf would come upon him by the light of the full moon. There had been woods in the movie, too.

There was no such thing as a werewolf! But there were great, big, hairy canine creatures that might very well come after a defenseless woman in the woods.

She wasn't defenseless. She was a New Yorker, and that had to count for something.

"Oh, God," she said. But it was true. She had nothing to defend herself with.

There came a rustling sound from the bushes.

Carly swallowed. Even if she knew in which direction she should be going, she couldn't walk. She still couldn't see, either.

She reached forward blindly. Groping, she found a long, splintered piece of wood.

Where was the driver? What the hell had happened
to him? she wondered irritably.

The wolf howled again. Carly let out a gasp, gripping her weapon more tightly. It was really just a splintered piece of wood, she thought dismally. Not strong
at all. If a rabid wolf came after her, it would probably
break in two seconds. But it was sharp, at least. It was
kind of a stake, she decided. A stake, like the kind used
to kill vampires.

Vampires.

"Oh!" she wailed. "Stop it!"

But there was a wolf out there. And it was coming
closer, circling around her, she thought.

And it was so dark. She could feel the mist about her,
soft and damp and swirling. There was another rustle
in the trees, right in front of her.

It was just the horses, she tried to tell herself.

No, she was sure she had heard them running away as
the carriage crashed and broke up.

Maybe they had come back.

No. Whatever moved toward her seemed to have
night vision. It came slowly, slyly. Furtively.

The cloud moved. Eerie moonlight lighted the copse
again. Carly looked up at the orb in the sky, then
gasped when she heard movement once more. She
looked across the copse, and her scream seemed to
freeze in her throat.

It was the wolf.

Huge and snarling, its yellow eyes fixed upon her.
The beast stood not twenty-five yards away. Saliva
dripped from its ivory fangs.

It would kill her, Carly thought. She had her little
stick; the wolf had sharp fangs. How much did the beast

weigh? she wondered. A hundred pounds? A hundred fifty pounds?

What did it matter? She herself was five foot four and not quite a hundred and ten pounds. The wolf could devour her in one swallow, or, at the very least, tear her to shreds.

If it was just a wolf.

A distant howl sounded; Carly decided that the woods were full of beasts. This one wanted her. To rip her limb from limb.

"No!" She shook her head to dispel the fantasy. If she weren't frozen by such sheer terror, her eyes locked with those of the wolf, she would have smiled at her imagination.

She had to realize that the wolf was as real as the careening carriage, and she had to fight it to save her life. But her weapon was so flimsy.

Still, she faltered to her feet, then carefully balanced her weight upon her good foot and raised her flimsy stick high above her head in what she thought was a threatening manner.

The wolf took a step toward her.

She knew not to run. A wolf was cousin to a dog, and Carly knew that running would only bring on a growling dog. Not that she could have run, anyway. But despite herself, when the wolf came forward, she stepped back, nearly screaming out at the pain that shot through her ankle.

The wolf came on again. Slowly. As if he could corner her.

And again, despite all the commands her mind gave her limbs, Carly took another step back.

This time she collided with something. Something massive and dark and living. Another scream catching in her throat, she whirled.

The moon passed behind the cloud again. Darkness filled the sky and the night.

And then the moon reappeared.

Carly discovered that she was looking up at a man. She had backed up against an immense horse, and astride the horse was a man. He wore a high-collared cape and sat the curiously still animal with a natural grace. His hair was as jet as the night, and his eyes...

They were the same golden glowing amber as those of the wolf. Striking eyes. So powerful that it was several seconds before she realized that they belonged to a ruggedly handsome face.

Carly tried to open her mouth to speak. The man smiled, then looked past her to the wolf. He stared at it hard, then spoke softly to the creature.

"Go, Vixen!"

The wolf whined, tucked its tail between its legs and hurried into the forest.

The man dismounted. His cape swept about him as he did so. When he stood before Carly, she realized that he was wearing a soft cotton shirt with fine lace sleeves, black velvet breeches, white hose and black buckled shoes. He was several inches over six feet, she guessed. His shoulders were broad, and he moved with the lithe grace of an athlete.

"Ms. Kiernan?" he said sharply.

Carly swallowed, finding it difficult to speak. He was dark and fascinating, and the mist swirling about their feet made her wonder if the man could be real.

"Yes," she managed to reply.

He smiled slowly. She thought it was the most sensual smile that she had ever seen. His smile was youthful, but his eyes were all knowing. They were hazel, she assured herself. A nice, normal hazel.

"You're hurt." His voice was husky and warm and deep. It entered her bloodstream and warmed her. There was a very slight accent to it, as if he spoke English without hesitation, as if he knew her. As if he had known that she would be here, alone and vulnerable in the misted woods.

He towered over her, and on this night in particular he left her in no little awe. She stared up into his eyes as if she were compelled to do so, and then realized what she was doing. Quickly she lowered her lashes.

"You're hurt," he repeated.

"No, no, not really—"

She broke off as he reached into her hair and removed a strand of dry grass. Self-consciously Carly moved her fingers through her hair. Her French braid had come loose. Half her tawny hair remained entwined; half of it spilled upon her shoulders. He stared deep into her eyes and gave her a crooked, rueful smile. Carly felt herself returning that stare, unable to turn away. She trembled slightly, feeling as if he touched her.

He was a stranger, a man who had appeared in the woods out of nowhere, she reminded herself. A silent wraith in the night. She felt warm and safe, though she was alone in the fog-drenched woods with him. She didn't know who he was, or where he had come from, only that he wore a cape and rode a black horse and had the power to make a wolf slink away from its prey.

At least he spoke English, she thought. Her French was sufficient when she was ordering food and wine; it would not carry her far in a political debate.

She could not tear her eyes from his, nor could she fight the feeling that she was warm and safe now, because he was here.

He broke the eye contact, looking beyond her to the ruins of the carriage. He stared at the wreckage, then back at her.

"My God! What happened?" he exclaimed huskily.

"I, uh, I'm not sure. Suddenly we were speeding, and then I realized that there was no driver, and then the carriage . . . crashed."

"You could have been killed."

There was a harsh sound to his voice; it had a deep timbre, and the concern in it seemed to touch her all over again.

"I'm all right," she told him.

"Where the hell is the driver?" he demanded.

"I—I don't know. I hope he isn't hurt."

"If he isn't hurt, then he should be horsewhipped." He stared at the wreckage again, still scowling. "My God," he murmured once more. His eyes, darkened by emotion, sought and held hers.

"I'm all right," she insisted. "Really. Thanks to you. I admit that I was quite frightened by the wolf."

"Ah . . . the wolf," he said softly, arching a brow. "Yes, well, the wolf is gone now."

Then the moon slipped behind a cloud again and darkness descended upon them. Carly couldn't see his face or his features; she was barely aware that he still stood before her in front of the sleek black horse. Just then a streak of lightning flashed across the sky, illuminating the night. Now she saw the stranger before her clearly. He seemed to tower over her. He was very dark, compelling with his striking good looks. There was something about him that was so starkly masculine that it added an aura of tension and sensuality to him. If he did touch her, Carly knew, she would tremble.

The lightning flashed again. Furiously, the black horse pawed the earth.

"Satan!" the man said sharply.

Satan, Carly thought fleetingly. How appropriate.

Would the horse listen to his command just as easily as the wolf had?

The black horse reared suddenly, then slammed down upon the earth. The stranger caught hold of Carly's bare shoulders and dragged her away from the horse's hooves.

She cried out as her weight was placed on her sore ankle.

"You're hurt!" the man observed.

"No, I—"

"You've been injured. Don't act like a fool. You screamed in pain."

"I'm—"

"It's going to pour. All Hallows' Eve—a good rainstorm is right in order. I've got to get you out of here."

"Wait! If you'll just listen to me! I was heading for the castle—"

"Don't worry. I'll take you there," he promised her softly. His eyes held hers again. For the life of her, Carly couldn't look away.

Nor for the life of her could she remember when she had met such a man. He infuriated her with his dictatorial manner, but he also fascinated her. He was both elegant in his costume and so crudely male that he made her shiver. Made her think of illicit things in a peripheral, forbidden section of her mind. Staring at him, she felt a blush cover her cheeks. No man had ever made her feel this way.

She was feeling things that she barely understood. She'd never known such a sexual attraction. It was the night, she assured herself. It was the mist and it was the wind, and it was the primal howling and prowling of the wolves in the darkness. It was something instinctive inside her that brought her to him, for she was alone in this world of danger and fantasy, alone with him and in his keeping.

It was like a spell, she told herself. When they reached the castle, when they were surrounded by people and lights, the spell would be broken.

"If you'll take my hand," she managed to whisper, "I'm sure I'll be able to walk."

He didn't take her hand. Instead, he stepped forward and swept her into his arms. She clung to him, her arms locked around his neck. And yet when his gaze fell upon her then, she blushed again. It was such an intimate hold. She could feel the warmth of his blood as it coursed through his body. She could feel his heartbeat.

And she knew he could feel and see her pulse. Her gown left bare her shoulders and soft cleavage. She was sure he saw the quick rise and fall of her breasts, and when his eyes met hers again, there were both enigma and truth there.

"This isn't necessary," she told him.

He grinned down at her, and she thought he knew all her weaknesses.

"I think that it is."

"And what you think always matters?" she parried.

"At the moment, yes, it does. Do you care to debate the subject with me?"

Finding no words, she chose to stare at him, hoping that a pretense of cool condemnation would duly chastise him.

It didn't seem to affect him in the least.

"You're cold," he said softly. "We will quickly warm you."

And he did warm her, with the mere tone and cadence of his words. The blood rushed through her. She felt a flush rise to her cheeks.

Lightning flashed across the sky once more. He started walking toward Satan. Another bolt rent the night air.

The black stallion reared again. Reared and bolted.

"Satan, you devil, you!" the stranger roared in anger. Carly felt the constriction of his arms, felt the power of him. He was all warmth and vitality. Her heart began to thunder. He was holding her so tightly. She reminded herself that she was on foreign soil, lost in the mist, more alone with this man than ever as the black stallion's hoofbeats faded.

He looked down at her. His eyes glimmered gold, and he smiled slowly. "It may take us time to get back."

"You could put me down."

"No, I don't think so."

It was preposterous, she thought. He wasn't going to release her. She could only hope that he was really—decently—trying to help her.

"Do you know where we are?" she asked. It was so odd to talk to a total stranger when that man was holding her in his arms. They were so intimate, and yet their conversation had to be so casual.

"Yes, I know where we are." He grinned wickedly, and for an uncanny moment he resembled the legendary Count of Darkness. "I know my way well. It will just take us a little longer to reach our objective. I'm afraid that I'm not as fleet as that monster of a stallion."

Carly swallowed, wondering why she felt as if he could have compelled the animal to return, had he truly desired to do so.

"Well, my lady," he murmured gallantly, falling into the role that her fine silk and velvet costume suggested. He started walking. He moved easily, as if her weight meant very little to him.

For a while they walked in silence. Carly keenly felt the mist. A wolf howled somewhere, and she tensed. The stranger tightened his arms around her, and she discovered his hypnotic eyes staring into hers again, his lips curled into a fascinating and wicked smile.

"You are safe, you know," he said.

Carly wasn't sure of what to say. Where he held her, she seemed to burn. Where he didn't touch her, she felt cold. She was struck with the intimacy of his hold and was amazed anew at her reaction to him. She had never easily fallen for a man.

But then, she had never met such a man. When she had loved, it had been slowly and deeply. She had never known this feeling of...excitement until love had found its roots within her.

Perhaps she had never been touched by someone like this. Someone who towered against the darkness of the night, vibrant, sure and strong. Someone who swept her into his arms without thought of asking permission. Someone who compelled her, frightened her, who fascinated her to no end....

Was this safety?

She had to get down. She could not let him hold her so intimately any longer.

"Please, really, you can't carry me all that way," she said.

He looked down at her and arched a deadly dark brow. He smiled again, slowly. They both knew he could carry her all night with little effort, if he so chose.

"I promise you, you're safe," he told her.

Perhaps, but safe from what? Certainly not from him . . .

Lightning came now in a sudden flash; thunder cracked ferociously. And suddenly rain fell. It was a soft patter at first but turned to a blinding flood.

He held her more closely against him. Water streamed down his strong features and clung to his lashes. He caught the corner of his cloak and swept that around her, using the breadth of his shoulders to protect her the best he could.

"I don't think we can make the castle in this!" he shouted over the rain. "I'm heading for the hunting lodge. All right?"

She sincerely doubted that she had a choice.

He turned off into the woods. When the moon fell behind the clouds, she couldn't see anything. She couldn't protest; she could barely move as he hurried along. The rain was hard and stinging. She opened her mouth once to speak, and it was instantly filled with water. Having little choice, Carly closed her mouth and her eyes and clung to him. Branches and twigs snapped and the foliage crackled beneath his feet as they hurried on.

In another flash of lightning, Carly saw that they had come to something at last. It was the hunter's cottage, made of hewn logs. She had hoped they would come upon people, but they didn't. The place was dark, and the absence of wires indicated there was no electricity.

He burst through the doorway. Carly was blinded by the darkness, but apparently he could see. Without faltering, he set her down upon something soft and dry and warm. She lay still, shivering. She heard his footsteps as he moved about. A second later, a candle gleamed from a bare wooden table in the center of the room. His face was eerie above that glow as he smiled at her.

"I'll build a fire," he promised. He came back over to her. She trembled as he touched her lower lip with his forefinger. "You're shivering. It will warm you and dry us, I hope."

Carly didn't speak as he moved away. She watched the easy way he hunkered down, his weight on the balls of his feet as he built a fire. Taking a long match from the narrow stone mantel above him, he touched the flame against several places.

At last, he seemed satisfied that the fire was catching. Though Carly could already feel the warmth that radiated from it, she shivered.

He rose, then swung around, sweeping the cape around him. She noticed again the jet black of his hair, the glowing gold of his eyes, the full sensuality of his mouth and the lean but powerful grace of his stance.

"Is that better?" he asked.

Carly nodded, still huddled upon the bed.

"I think I can make it even better than that," he assured her. He left the mantel and walked to the other side of the room. There was an old well pump there, a sink and a number of cabinets above a counter. He reached into the cabinets and produced glasses and a bottle of brandy.

"Do you—know the owner?" Carly asked. She should be nervous, she told herself. She shouldn't feel so comfortable and so easy with this strange man in this strange place. He was dressed as Dracula, and he might as well have been that elusive demon, for it seemed his power over her was as great as that of the legendary Count over the young women he seduced.

He paused, smiling slowly as he looked at her a moment. He set the glasses down and poured brandy into each. "Yes, I know the owner," he told her.

He walked over to her, offering the brandy. She took the glass. He raised his. "A toast, *mademoiselle*. You are a *demoiselle* this evening, no? A lady of Napoleon's court?"

Carly smiled. "I was."

He stood over her. His wet shirt and breeches hugged his body. She looked up into his eyes and raised her glass to touch it to his. "Cheers, *monsieur*. You've done all this and we're not even properly introduced. Well, you knew my name. I'm here with my sister, Jasmine, for the Vadim's ball. Well, I'm not with Jasmine. I'm looking for her. She should be at the ball."

"Ah, I see." He offered her no more information. He stood there, and she was keenly aware of him as a man again, disturbingly aware of the body the wet clothing clung to—the lean, masculine hips, the long well-muscled legs.

She looked back into his eyes, his compelling amber eyes. He moved away from her, walking toward the fire, which was growing steadily to a sure blaze.

Carly swallowed her brandy. It burned her throat, then warmed her belly and limbs. He tilted back his head and swallowed his brandy and set the glass on the mantel. He turned around to face her. He was purely arresting there, tall and powerful and supremely confident, supremely male.

He smiled, a smile that was both wicked and amused.

She was no easily frightened child, Carly knew. She was a mature woman who knew how to deal with life and death and men. Even this one, she assured herself.

But still the tremors raced through her.

Seated upon a quilt-covered bunk with her toes curled beneath her, Carly straightened her shoulders. She returned his smile with a slightly arrogant one of her own, her brow arched. "Who are you?" she asked bluntly.

He moved away from the mantel, picking up the brandy bottle from the counter. He came back over to her and poured a second measure into her glass. She had to will herself to hold it steady. When he was finished, his eyes met hers.

"I am the count," he said.

She smiled. "Vlad Dracul, yes, I can see that. Your costume is wonderful. I meant who are you really?"

His smile deepened. "The count, *mademoiselle*."

Carly frowned. "The count—"

"Count Vadim, Ms. Kiernan. I am Count Jon Vadim."

He kept his eyes locked upon her. The fire rose and crackled, and the room seemed to be ablaze. Carly wanted to tear her gaze from his but could not.

He touched her chin, caressing it lightly with his palm and callused fingers. "Welcome to Westphalen, Carly Kiernan."

Carly felt his touch, and her flesh caught fire. She wondered vaguely if she hadn't already lost her sanity, her soul.

So this was Count Vadim.

She had been warned about him.

Jasmine had warned her....

His smile suddenly seemed cold. "All right. Fantasy time is over, Ms. Kiernan. So now tell me. Just who are you really, and what the hell do you want here?"

Chapter 2

Carly wrenched herself away from his touch. His eyes could be very hard, she thought. Cold, glittering amber, like the wolf's.

"I'm exactly who I say I am," she told him flatly. "And if you're the count, you damn well know it."

"Well, I damned well do not," he snapped back. "Jasmine isn't here. She hasn't been here. If you were her sister, you would know that."

"But Jasmine is here! And I am her sister! I just received a letter from her."

He shook his head, staring at her. "No. You're mistaken. Jasmine decided that she didn't want to stay for the ball. She's gone. You're here, so you might as well come for the evening. But then you've got to go home."

"Without Jasmine? You're crazy!"

He could be a lot worse than crazy, she thought. She had to keep in mind where she was: in the mists of mysterious forests and mountains where creatures roamed, where wolves lurked....

No, no, no. The evening was making her into a lunatic!

By the light of the full moon...

Carly couldn't remember what else went with the line, but she could imagine a score of movies in which the gypsy fortune-teller warned the unwary that danger lurked here, along with the full moon.

So far she had been in the wreck of an eighteenth-century carriage and met a wolf—and a count. And her sister was missing.

What more could she ask for?

"I'm not going anywhere, Count Vadim. My sister wrote me a letter from your castle. I will not go anywhere until I have her with me again!"

Sighing, he walked away, then returned to her. "Look, you know Jasmine. Here today, gone tomorrow. You've barely been here an evening, and already you've been hurt. You need to leave."

"No. Not until I find Jasmine. Or not until you can tell me exactly where she is."

"You stubborn little—" he began, then laughed suddenly and took her chin again. He didn't hurt her, but his hold was strong. She didn't try to wrench away. Her heart was pounding, her breath came too quickly, and deep inside, she was trembling.

"I am Jasmine's sister."

He sighed. "You're not supposed to be here."

"She wrote to me—"

"Yes, yes. But you must go home."

"No."

"You are a stubborn little creature!"

He studied her with grave care. Some gentler emotion suddenly flashed into his eyes, and there was an intriguing blend of tenderness and mischief about his gaze as he touched her cheek and chin—too intimately she thought.

It was a little too much like hypnotism, she decided. He seduced, and perhaps he did not demand blood, but Carly was afraid it could be far too easy to lose her heart.

She was a survivor, she reminded herself. Tough and resilient. She lived in New York by choice. She could handle Transylvanian nobility. No problem.

She caught his fingers and removed them from her face. "What did you have in mind? We can't even seem to reach the castle, and you'd like to put me on a 747." Carly decided to make practical use of his nearness, so she held his hand, mindful of the electricity of his touch, and staggered to her feet.

"You can stay for the ball," he said, "and you can stay the night."

"Thank you. I have a hotel room."

"That won't be necessary. You can stay at the castle. It will only be for the night."

"I'll stay at the hotel. And I'll stay as long as I choose."

He smiled suddenly. "Are you afraid of me, Ms. Kiernan?"

"No."

"Perhaps you should be."

"Why?"

"We both know the answer to that," he replied.

"I'm so sorry, count. But I don't."

"All right, then. Good. If you're not afraid of me, come to the castle."

"But I'm not going home tomorrow," she insisted.

"We'll see."

"I want to see Jasmine."

"Jasmine is a damned butterfly! Who knows where the hell she has decided to alight!"

Carly lowered her eyes. "We're going in circles," she murmured.

His attitude changed abruptly and he laughed suddenly, as if it all were a great joke. He finished his brandy, poured himself another shot, and turned around to study her again.

"So you are Jasmine's little sister."

"Yes, I'm Jasmine's sister, but little? We're not even a year apart." She tried to hobble toward the fire and winced as she put weight on her foot.

"Don't step on it," he warned her. There was a bench before the fire, and he helped her to it. The feeling of his arms about her was curiously natural. Even while they argued, she fought the urge to touch him. She would have loved this to be sheer fantasy, a world in which she could close her eyes, shut out the light, fall into his arms and follow wherever he might lead.

Yet she really hadn't stumbled into a fantasy, and none of this was imagination. This was the twentieth century. He was wearing an expensive after-shave that she recognized as one that had only recently reached an exclusive market.

Once she was seated, he knelt down before her. Carly stared down at his dark head as he examined her ankle.

"How well do you and Jasmine know each other?" she asked carefully. Jasmine was the one who had warned her. Was she treading, if only by a curious twist of fate, upon her sister's territory?

He paused a moment, then shrugged. "Well enough. She's a clever and enterprising young woman."

"Yes, that's Jasmine," Carly said.

"And she is a butterfly."

"She's lively. I'm worried about her."

"You shouldn't be." He looked up at her. "I must have some kind of a pot here. If I can heat some water, you can soak your foot, and perhaps by the time someone comes for us it will be somewhat better."

"Do you think someone will come for us?"

"Yes," he said. "I rode down to find you when you didn't appear. Someone will come soon."

He rose, returned to the counter and dug beneath it until he produced a large pot. He filled it from the pump and hung it from an old-fashioned spit over the fire.

"It will heat quickly," he told Carly.

Crouched by the fire, he watched her again. Firelight caught his eyes, and they gleamed golden upon her.

"The designer," he murmured, sweeping his gaze over her sodden costume.

"Jasmine told you about me?"

"Yes—but apparently not enough."

"Meaning?..."

"Well, I had no idea that you were coming here. Not until you called this afternoon."

"Why didn't you want to see me?"

"Because..." He paused and shrugged. "Because Jasmine isn't here," he said. Carly wondered what he was hiding from her.

He smiled, and she thought that it was a wonderful smile. He was such a contradiction—cold and hard one moment, curiously tender the next.

"A designer—and a very good one," he said. "Despite the damage it has received this evening, your dress is still stunning."

"Thank you." Carly frowned suddenly. "Your accent is British."

"Is it?"

"Of course it is," she told him suspiciously.

He laughed, and she thought it had a disdainful tone to it. "French is our official language, Ms. Kiernan. We don't all learn American English in Europe. British accents are much more common here."

"But there is no French accent in your speech!" she said, ignoring the intended insult.

"And there is no English accent in my French," he said with annoyance. He sighed, staring back into her eyes, which delved with a dead-set challenge into his. "My mother is—was—British."

"Oh," Carly murmured. She was disappointed; she thought she had caught him in something. At her obvious chagrin, he smiled again. Then he touched her cheek with a gesture that was almost a caress and moved his fingers over her bodice.

"You are very, very good. The dress is wonderful. You create a fantasy within it. You could be Désirée, the innocent young beauty who first stole Napoleon's heart."

"She was dark, I believe," Carly said.

"Perhaps. And you are a golden blonde with turquoise eyes and a delicate heart-shaped face. But you're very talented. I am sure that you will go wherever you want with your artistry."

"Jasmine has been talking."

"Jasmine is loyal and enthused."

"Yes, she is." Carly felt a pang of jealousy of her sister, along with new worry. Where was Jasmine, and just how well had she come to know this fascinating stranger?

This was, she thought, just the type of thing that Jasmine would do. Fall in love with an exotic count and run off to Romania, of all places.

Except that the count, though an overwhelming and striking man, didn't seem strange or exotic. He was built like a football player but had the manners of an Englishman.

"Not quite George Hamilton," she remarked.

"I beg your pardon," he said to her.

She laughed. "Well, if I'm to be Désirée, I should try to figure out your costume."

He grinned broadly. "Count Dracula, who else?"

"Yes, but which?" Carly teased. "Suave—George Hamilton. Hypnotic—Bela Lugosi." She paused, then smiled and added, "Armand Assante—incredibly sexy. Then there's Chris Sarandon—young and striking."

He laughed and took her hand between his two palms. He smoothed his fingers over hers and smiled warmly. "From you, *mam'selle*," he teased her softly, "I will gladly accept them all."

The fire crackled, rose and flamed around them. Carly stared into his eyes, and a sweet heat filled her. This might have been the world, the entire world, this little log cottage in the misted mountains where the fire burned so warmly....

And this man knelt before her, touching her. She could think of nothing but the excitement that seemed to fill her with liquid magic, golden tremors. In her life she'd had but one love. She'd never really dated; she'd married straight out of high school, and after she had lost him, she'd indulged in nothing more serious than proper dinner or theater dates.

And now she knew that she wanted this man to hold her, to kiss her. She wanted to be alone with him in the cabin forever, and she wanted to feel the fire against her bare flesh and his.

Too much brandy! an inner voice warned her. Maybe so, she thought, because she looked straight at him and asked, "Are you having an affair with my sister?"

He stared back at her. His answer seemed a long time coming, but despite that, she believed him. "No."

Carly nodded slowly. "*Did* you have an affair with my sister?"

"Did I?. . ." He paused, then with a rueful half curl to his lip said, "Did the man here before you now have an affair with your sister? Never. I swear it."

She lowered her eyes. He caught her chin and murmured, "I'd love to have you stay."

"You've been practically throwing me back across the ocean."

"Because you should go home. It isn't what I want. It would just be better for you."

"Why?" she asked.

"Maybe it is dangerous for you to be here."

"Where's the danger? Wolves in the forest?"

"Maybe," he said ruefully. "Maybe wolves—not in the forest."

She laughed, then lowered her head again. He touched her hair. "Jasmine's sister. You are beautiful."

She flushed. But it was true. She wanted him, as a man. And if she lost her soul in the bargain, well, so be it. The emotion was so strong that it was shattering, and yet it felt good to her. It was vital, and it was alive.

"I think the water is hot," he said. He took the pot from the fire. He gently removed the satin slipper she was wearing. Carly somewhat awkwardly removed her stocking and hastily set her foot into the water.

She jerked it back out, nearly screaming. The water was scalding. Startled, Count Vadim leaped to his feet and caught her when she would have fallen.

He didn't let her go. He held her in his arms, watching her eyes. "I think we let the water heat too long," he said.

"Yes, I think so, too."

Then he kissed her.

His lips fell upon hers, molding to them. She found herself enveloped, the damp black cloak engulfing them both. Though the material that lay between them was still damp, too, it didn't matter. It seemed that their bodies fused with the contact. He was hard and lean, and she could feel the firm ripple of his muscled chest, where her breasts pressed against it. His mouth was fire as it moved against hers, molding and meeting, both so gentle and so commanding that he swept her away with it. He made love with his mouth. It ravaged and plundered, then moved softly, only to ravage again. Carly discovered herself clinging to him, running her fingers desperately through his hair. His tongue entered her mouth with its magic and embedded a growing desire deep inside her. He tasted her lips and explored her teeth. She and the count were frozen in that time and space, aware of only each other and of the abiding beauty of a first kiss. Their eyes met, they kissed again, and Carly had no idea of where things might go from there. At that moment, she thought, she could have done anything and welcomed it. She would have gladly removed the Empire gown and felt the firelight upon her naked flesh. She would have gladly watched him cast aside his clothes and seen him glimmer, too, before that fire as he walked into her arms.

But he moved away from her suddenly, and his eyes were enigmatic as he stared at her. He smiled and touched her lips.

"They're here," he said softly.

"What?" Carly murmured.

"They've come for us."

There was a rapping at the door. "Jon! Are you in there?"

Jon Vadim strode to the door and opened it. Carly saw a man and a woman there. He was dressed as a mummy; she was a cat.

"Yes, Geoff, I'm here," Jon said. "And I have Ms. Kiernan, Jasmine's sister."

"Thank God!" said the man.

"Why? What's the matter?"

"Jon, no one can find the coachman. He's simply disappeared. We called the police as soon as you left, and they started out on the road. The poor man simply isn't to be found. We were so worried. I thought you might have come here."

"You thought right," Jon said. "Mummy dearest, come here. Geoffrey Taylor, Jasmine's sister, Carly Kiernan."

The mummy stepped into the room, offering Carly a swaddled hand. She couldn't tell what Geoffrey really looked like, since he was covered in frightfully real and musty-looking wrappings.

"Your costume is fabulous," she said.

"I am," he remarked.

He surveyed her with warm brown eyes. "And so is your Josephine," he observed. "Jasmine tells me that you've designed for a number of off-Broadway shows."

"Yes, I have."

"I'd like to talk over the next few weeks. I can see you know your business."

"She won't be here for the next few weeks," Jon said.

"Yes, I will be around," Carly corrected him. "Until I can find Jasmine."

"Jasmine?" The mummy looked over at Jon. "I thought Jasmine was off to Paris or somewhere else for the holiday."

Jon lifted his hands. "She's off somewhere. Carly doesn't believe me."

"Well, that's a shame," the woman interjected. "Jasmine is gone, and the damned party will be gone, too! It's already being ruined terribly!" She spoke in a bored and petulant voice that had a very proper English accent.

Carly watched as the woman, who made a very sleek and shapely cat, stepped forward. Carly didn't think she'd ever seen a costume so well calculated to display in the most flattering way the assets of a woman's anatomy.

"Tanya, meet Carly," Jon Vadim said dryly. "Carly, Tanya Bannister."

Tanya barely nodded. "Such a commotion!" she complained.

"And with good reason," Jon said. "The carriage is in ruins. I don't know what happened to the driver, but we're quite lucky that Carly wasn't hurt—or killed."

"Of course," Tanya said.

Carly realized that the woman couldn't care less whether she was dead or alive, just as long as she could get back to her party. Tanya stepped up to Jon and linked her arm through his.

"But Carly is all right. Can't we please get back to the castle? We never have the opportunity in London to see a group like the A.J.'s. I want to hear them play," Tanya fairly purred, her fingers resting on Jon Vadim's arm. He smiled at her, and Carly thought that Tanya's fake tail was about to swish with satisfaction.

"Tanya," Jon said, "I have to kill the fire—"

"But I need to talk to you! For just a moment," she said.

"I'll walk you back to the car—"

"I'll kill the fire," Geoffrey offered.

"Jon, it's very important," Tanya insisted.

Jon appeared irritated. He glanced Carly's way, and she smiled sweetly. "Please, you two go on out. I've been so looking forward to meeting Geoffrey."

"Let's go, Tanya. Make it brief."

He had her out the door quickly. Geoff gazed at Carly and grinned. "She *is* a cat," he said. "Equipped with claws and fangs, I think."

"So it seems," Carly agreed. "But whose cat is she?"

Geoffrey shrugged, seeming uncomfortable. "I really am anxious to talk. I'm so surprised that Jasmine isn't here. She was eager for the two of us to get together, you know." He walked over to the fireplace and poked the logs apart, then stooped to dig sand out of a black pot to kill the flames. He glanced back at Carly and offered her a lopsided mummy smile.

"Yes, Jasmine was eager for us to meet," Carly said. "And I'm worried about her."

"Don't be," he soothed her. "You must know Jasmine. She moves with the night wind, does whatever takes her fancy."

"Yes, I know, but..." But she wouldn't have invited me here, Carly thought. She wouldn't have written the words "I need you."

"Well, we will talk, and I am very impressed. You do plan to stay awhile," he said.

"Yes."

"No matter what Jon has to say?" He said this with a smile, but she found it difficult to tell what he was thinking, with his face obscured.

"No matter what anyone says," she replied firmly. "If Jasmine is off somewhere, she'll know she can reach me here."

"Well, that seems to be about it. Let's get going, shall we?"

He opened the door for her. Jon and Tanya Bannister were just outside in the damp night. Their heads were close, and Carly wondered what they were whispering about.

She felt a bit like a fool. There was no reason Jon Vadim shouldn't have close... acquaintances. But first she'd been concerned about his relationship with Jasmine, and he'd denied any involvement with her sister. Now Carly was wondering, though she tried to resist, about the beautiful but selfish Tanya.

"We're all set," Geoffrey announced cheerfully.

Carly kept a smile on her face and tried not to look at Jon. She had no rights here. She had just met the man, and perhaps she was really just proving her naiveté about the ways of the world—or of the international jet set, at least.

The kiss that she had shared with Jon had been special to her, had seduced her to the point where she'd longed to make love with a man she barely knew.

Carly shook her head. Where was her customary common sense?

"What car did you bring?" Jon asked Geoffrey.

"The Volvo."

"It's a good thing Jasmine isn't here," Tanya remarked sweetly to Carly. "She just hates the Volvo."

"Does she?" Carly said coolly.

"The Lamborghini is her car," Tanya said. She smiled, and swirled around, swishing her cat's tail as she started down a dark path that led to the road, where Carly could just barely see the shape of an automobile.

Jasmine wasn't like that! she wanted to scream.

Then she realized that she'd really barely seen Jasmine for some time. Her sister had stopped by Carly's apartment in early September to be fitted for the harem outfit, then later in the month to pick up the costume. Other than that, Jasmine had been traveling. She didn't have to conduct any of her tours; she had well-trained, well-paid employees for that. But she was a wonderful guide and really seemed to love the world. She'd built up a clientele among the noble, the rich and the famous, and everyone knew that the tours Jasmine herself led would always be the best.

Carly was brought out of her reverie by the plaintive cry of the wolf. Ahead of Carly on the trail, Tanya cried, "Those wolves!"

"I thought you liked wolves!" Geoffrey called out to her.

Carly watched as Tanya turned around and cast him an evil glare. Then she screamed suddenly. Someone had stepped out from the foliage and onto the trail.

"Alexi!" Tanya gasped.

"Tanya! I'm sorry—"

"Alexi, you scared me to death!"

"Tanya, I'm so sorry! I didn't mean to scare you. I just wanted to see if Jon had found Jasmine's sister. Ah! I see that he has."

"Yes, he has," Jon said, stepping past Carly. He caught her hand and pulled her forward.

Alexi was a handsome young man with wavy brown hair in a twenties mob-style pin-striped suit. He smiled at Tanya and at Jon and looked at Carly with undisguised curiosity and a naked admiration that flattered her despite herself.

"So this is the sister," he said in a heavy accent. "Sister Carly, it is pleasure!"

Carly noticed that he had brown eyes and a charming, boyish smile.

"This is Alexi Moreau," Jon told her. "He's a neighbor of mine. He has a wonderful old family manor quite near the castle."

"You will see it," Alexi Moreau assured Carly.

"Will I? Thank you so very much."

She felt Jon Vadim's fingers tighten around her arm as he said, "If you wish, Carly, I will take you there."

"Come with me now," Alexi suggested. "I've brought the Mercedes."

"She'll come with me," Jon insisted with quiet but undeniable force. Carly, again, felt flattered, but she was bound to resist him. "Actually, I—"

"The Mercedes," Tanya said, interrupting her. "Let's all go back in it, and someone can pick up the Volvo tomorrow. Please, let's get back to the party!"

"I'm sure the party is still in full swing," Jon said. "But Tanya is right. We should get back."

Carly found herself in the back of the Mercedes with Jon Vadim and Geoffrey, while Tanya rode with Alexi.

In the darkness of the car, Jon Vadim reached over for Carly's hand and closed his warm, strong fingers around hers. Then he leaned forward, pointing into the distance.

"Castle Bran lies that way, just over the border. They call it Dracula's castle, though Vlad Tepes had little to do with the place. We'll go there tomorrow."

"Vlad Tepes?" Carly murmured.

"Vlad the Impaler," Alexi supplied.

"Actually," Jon said, his eyes wickedly aglitter in the darkness, "Dracula is not so much a name as a description. It means 'son of the dragon.' His father's name was Vlad, too."

"But he was never a vampire," Alexi said.

"No, he was much, much worse. He was known to execute up to thirty thousand people at one time. To others he was quite a hero, for he despised the Turks and kept them at bay. But once, he was angered by the people of Brasov, the village down in the valley—we'll go there, too. Well, the villagers refused to submit to his command. He solved the problem by doing away with them. Men, women and children—he impaled them all."

"With a very special finesse," Alexi interjected cheerfully.

"Ah, yes. When impaling a man, he took great care not to hit any vital organs. It would take two or three days for the poor victim to bleed to death."

"That's horrible!" Carly exclaimed.

"Terribly cruel," Jon said amiably.

"Stop it!" Tanya cried with a shudder. "You're frightening me. You're—frightening Carly!"

Carly felt Jon's eyes on her, though she didn't look his way.

"I'm not frightened," Carly insisted, then she turned to look at him. He was indeed watching her.

He smiled slowly, almost challengingly, then said, "No, I don't think you are."

"Not of the past," she added.

"No, of course not." He still held her hand. His knee brushed hers, and she felt the warmth of him. "You would fear only the wolf that you could see, in the here and now, right?"

"Right," Carly said.

"And do you see a wolf, here and now?" he asked.

"No." She spoke firmly, without hesitation. His smile deepened, and she didn't know if he was pleased or disappointed.

"That's good," he said lightly. "In this place it is not wise to give way to fantasy or to the power of imagination."

"The people still believe," Alexi murmured from the driver's seat.

Carly caught his brown gaze in the rearview mirror.

"You will see, Carly, that our villages have changed little since the Middle Ages. The people hang crosses upon their doors to ward away evil. And along the very road we travel there are many shrines to protect travelers from the dangers of the night."

"Pity I didn't stumble upon any of the shrines," Carly said with a laugh. "I stumbled upon a—"

"There." Jon Vadim interrupted her almost curtly. "There—we have reached the castle."

Alexi drove through a massive iron gate that broke the outer walls.

Up close, Castle Vadim was far more awe-inspiring than frightening. It was built of some native stone, and seeming to rise straight out of the rock, it was harsh and gray, yet it was graceful, too, for it boasted turrets and towers and parapets. Arrow slits were the only openings in the tower rooms, but on the ground level, the edifice had been brought into the twentieth century with reconstruction. Great picture windows enclosed an elegant terrace where couples swayed and danced to a hard rock band.

"Well?" Jon Vadim said. Carly felt his gaze on her again.

She stared up at the castle, then turned and smiled at him. "It's—it's magnificent," she said.

"It's intriguing," he said softly, then helped Carly alight from the car. She looked down ruefully at her soaked gown.

"I'm a mess."

"You are a mess, sweetie," Tanya agreed. "I'll just take Carly upstairs, Jon, and dry her out a bit."

He nodded, watching Carly.

"Come on," Tanya urged her. "You'll get a better tour later. For now, we'll just hurry."

They didn't enter by way of the terrace. Tanya led Carly up a flight of worn and narrow stone steps to an arched doorway, then pushed open a massive nail-studded door.

A dim hallway attractively decorated with old swords and shields and coats of arms led to a wide, curving stairway. "This way," Tanya encouraged her.

At the top of the stairs they entered another room. It was ancient, but a rug lay before the hearth, the massive brass bed was covered with a quilt, and a silver tea service was set on an occasional table. On a matching table on the other side of the fireplace was a television set.

Carly noticed an overnight bag on the bed. The mirrored dresser to the left of the bed was strewn with brushes and makeup.

"You've been staying here?" Carly asked casually.

"Of course," Tanya replied. "The place is huge. Geoff stays here, I stay here, Jasmine stays here. He could have twenty guests at a time if he wanted. Of course, Jasmine—" She broke off, shrugging.

"Of course Jasmine what?" Carly demanded.

"Nothing. I thought she'd finally caught the elusive count, that's all. And then she leaves. Who knows?" Tanya shrugged again, then, to Carly's surprise, smiled. "Sit down. I'll get the blow dryer."

"That's okay Tanya. I can manage."

"Come on, please! I know I come on a little strong. I'm just not a hypocrite, that's all. I have a little sister, too. Let me give you a hand."

Carly sat on the bed, and Tanya set to work with the hair dryer.

"Now stand up," Tanya commanded at last. "I'll dry your dress."

"What?"

"It will work. I swear it," Tanya promised.

And actually, it did. Carly still felt a little squishy inside, but she was able to stand before the mirror and admit that she didn't look much different from the way she had when she'd left the hotel in the ill-fated carriage.

"There! As good as new," Tanya insisted with pleasure. "Now, let's go downstairs. There's a party going on." She smiled.

Carly decided that Tanya was still a cat, but an honest cat, and she was really okay as long as her claws were sheathed. "Thanks for the help," she said.

"No problem. We'll take the grand stairway this time," Tanya told her.

The stairway was indeed grand, carved completely from oak and covered with a maroon velvet runner. It swept down in dual outward curves. To the rear were family portraits that Carly saw dated from the Middle Ages.

"This is fabulous," she whispered. "It's almost decadent!"

Tanya cast her a quick glance, then laughed. "You would think so, I guess. Come on, will you?"

Tanya dragged her down the stairway and around the corner. The rotunda opened onto the terrace. A tuxedoed servant came by with a silver tray full of champagne glasses. Carly scooped up two and handed one to Tanya.

"Oh! There are the Seybolds!" Tanya said. "You must meet them. They're friends of Jasmine's. He'll be a candidate in the next presidential race. And that's Lord Bowden with them—he's in the British parliament. The Marquis de Grasse...the de Grasses are in wine these days—no money in just being noble..."

It seemed to Carly that Tanya had adopted her for the evening. Carly met a charming Russian diplomat, a dime store heiress, a tire king and dozens of politicians. They were dressed as princes and princesses, monsters and ghouls, fruit, vegetables, cats, dogs and astronauts. Carly danced with a frog who assured her he was really a Lithuanian prince. She found herself in high demand and was very glad, because they all spoke so admiringly of Jasmine. And they all expressed surprise that Jasmine had not stayed in the duchy for the party.

Carly didn't realize that through it all she had been looking for someone—until he found her. She was still in the arms of the frog prince when she espied Jon Vadim. He was in the midst of a crowd, but his gaze was on her, with no apology. When he caught her eye, he set down his champagne glass, murmured something to his other guests, and came her way.

He cut in on the frog prince just as the rock band began to play a Viennese waltz. Carly slipped into his arms. Jon stared deeply, penetratingly into her eyes. He held her close and he whirled her around the room.

"Are you enjoying yourself?" he asked.

"Yes. Tremendously."

"I wasn't. Not until this moment."

Carly arched a brow. "Is that a line?"

"No. It's the truth. I swear it."

She smiled with a shrug.

"Do you believe in fate, Carly?" he asked. "In destiny, in things that were meant to be?"

She paused. Her feet were responding to the music and she was painfully aware of the simple thrill of being in his arms. What had happened to her? she wondered. This was not real, not the man, not the castle.

And she was shivering and trembling. She wanted to know him, wanted to feel his eyes upon her forever, wanted to stay in his arms forever, dancing beneath a full moon.

"I don't usually believe in fate," she replied finally. "I do believe, however, that you're a busy, busy man."

"Cruel blow, lady. And not true."

"Everyone seems to think that you and Jasmine were quite an item."

"I told you the truth," he stated firmly.

"Then there's the matter of a lovely little cat."

"Wolves and cats just don't get along. You should know that," he parried.

"Really?" She cast her head back and smiled. "Wolves prefer innocent lambs. Is that it?"

"Are you such an innocent lamb?"

"I can take care of myself."

"Good. I'll feel no guilt."

"About what?"

He ignored the question, smiling at her and saying, "I imagine..."

"Just what do you imagine?"

"I imagine, Carly, that your trust is hard to earn. That you do not fall in and out of love, but when you do, you do so deeply. I imagine that when you believe in someone, you do so with all your heart. And perhaps your faith will be unshakable."

She smiled, shaking her head. "I don't understand you."

"How could you?" he murmured.

More than ever she felt the mystery of the night. First Jasmine and now Jon Vadim.

"Jon..." Her voice faded as she realized that he was no longer looking at her. Still holding her, he stopped dancing and frowned as he looked past her to the terrace entrance.

"What is it?" she asked.

"Why, it's the inspector. Inspector LaRue. Excuse me."

Jon made to leave her there, but she followed. She watched as the two men shook hands then the newcomer spoke swiftly. Count Vadim's brows knitted.

"Jon, what is it?" Carly repeated, coming up behind him.

"Carly—"

"Good evening," the inspector interrupted quietly, reaching out to shake her hand, too.

He was a slim man with a drooping mustache and sad eyes. He seemed proud of his English, Carly thought.

"Madame Kiernan?"

"Yes."

"He found the coachman, Carly. Dead," Jon told her gently.

"Oh! How terrible!" she exclaimed. "Did he fall from the box at that speed? Oh, the poor man."

"Yes, the poor, poor man," the inspector agreed.

"He didn't fall," Jon Vadim said. He looked at Carly, his eyes seeming to pierce her as if he sought something.

"He was murdered. His throat was slit."

Chapter 3

It had to be the longest night of her life, Carly thought.

The party went on, but she and the count were absent, closeted with the inspector in the library. The inspector first questioned a number of the count's servants and dismissed them. Then he wanted to talk to Jon and Carly, Geoffrey, Alexi—and a very irritated Tanya. Poor Tanya wasn't destined to see much of the band, Carly mused.

The inspector was very polite; he didn't want to ruin the party. Tourism was big business in the duchy; he appreciated the financial aspects of Count Vadim's party. But he had to speak to them all, he had to ask questions, he was very sorry, and he hoped that they understood.

It was mainly Carly and the count he talked to. She could dimly hear the band playing as the inspector asked her again and again to tell him about the carriage ride from beginning to end. Jon leaned against his desk with his arms crossed over his chest and listened with a frown, occasionally warning the inspector that he was being rude to an American guest. He assured the inspector that he had hired the village man to drive merely because extra help had been needed for the party and the man had needed the extra money. He had barely known the man.

"All of this over a coachman!" Tanya complained with a sniff. "Inspector, you should see to the village drunks!"

"The village is not full of ignorant drunkards, Miss Bannister," the inspector said irritably.

"But perhaps the man did have enemies among his neighbors," Carly suggested.

"Anything is possible," Jon Vadim murmured.

"Madame Kiernan. I don't suppose you have any enemies in Westphalen," the inspector remarked dryly.

"Please!" Tanya groaned. "Carly has never even been here before!"

The inspector looked at Tanya. "I find it difficult to comprehend the murder of a simple village man. Here we have little in the way of drugs, robbery—or murder. Someone meant to hurt Madame Kiernan, I believe. Or perhaps to hurt someone through her. You, miss? Or the Vadims? One or the other, I am certain."

"I really don't know anyone here," Carly assured him. "I just came in from Vienna this evening."

The inspector nodded, glancing around the room. "Where were you all this evening when the coachman was killed and the carriage burst apart?"

"Oh, no!" Tanya complained. "I don't believe this! Some yokel gets himself killed and the entire party is ruined!"

"We were here at the party," Jon said.

"Well, no, that's not quite true," Alexi said guiltily, looking around at all of them. "Well...we were worried, you see. Jon had told us that he had hired a driver to pick up Jasmine's sister. When she didn't arrive, Jon left on Satan to look for Ms. Kiernan—"

"Jasmine!" Carly whispered suddenly.

"What?" The inspector narrowed his eyes upon her.

"Actually, Inspector, I am concerned," Carly told him. "You see, I came here to meet my sister. I arrived, and she wasn't here."

The inspector looked at Jon. Carly could have sworn that a slight sheen of perspiration broke out on Jon's brow, but he spoke smoothly and with a certain impatience. "Jasmine, Inspector. Jasmine Michaelson is Ms. Kiernan's sister. You've met her."

"And you say that your sister has disappeared?" the inspector asked Carly.

"She isn't here," she replied flatly, staring at Jon Vadim. He returned her stare, then gave her a slow smile.

"I have told Carly that Jasmine just isn't here. I believe that she went on to Paris, but I don't know."

"How can you possibly be worried about Jasmine!" Tanya said with exasperation. "She goes where she likes when she pleases!"

"But she wrote to me!" Carly protested. "She said 'Please come'! She said that she needed me!"

The inspector sighed. Geoffrey, whose mummy wrappings were peeling by now, came over to Carly and put his arm around her. "Jasmine is incredibly independent, you know," he reassured her.

"Yes, but she was involved in this party—"

"Jasmine involves herself in many things and then leaves them," he said quietly.

Carly bit her lip, wondering if Geoffrey might have been one of those "things" that Jasmine had involved herself with and then left behind.

"You said your sister sent you a letter," the inspector began again. "You don't by any chance have it, do you?"

"Yes!" Carly said. "It's in my little evening bag. I left it upstairs in Tanya's room. Shall I get it?"

"I'll go," Tanya offered, then grimaced. "You don't know the place that well yet. I'll—"

"Never mind," Jon said, interrupting her. "I'll send the maid." He pressed a buzzer on his desk and a moment later a maid appeared. After he spoke to her quickly in French, she bobbed a little curtsy and left them.

"Now, let's get back to the coachman, shall we," the inspector said. "Count Vadim, did you leave here this evening alone to find Madame Kiernan?"

"Alone," Jon responded flatly.

"We followed him quickly," Tanya said indignantly.

" 'We'?"

"Geoffrey and I."

"And you were always together?"

"Well, no, of course not. We were searching," she explained.

"And what about Alexi?"

"I came after the two of them," Alexi himself answered.

"So you were alone, too."

"Yes, I suppose so."

"Which of us would want to kill a coachman!" Tanya protested.

The inspector threw up his arms. "All right. That is all for this evening." He wagged a finger at Tanya. "But something more is going on here than the pathetic murder of a poor servant. I will find out what it is.''

"Inspector," Jon Vadim said sharply, "I'm sure Tanya is every bit as distressed as the rest of us.''

"Yes, yes, of course," the inspector said wryly.

Tanya flushed. "Well, of course I'm upset. I just don't see where any of us can possibly be involved." She smiled sweetly at the inspector. "Aren't you going to warn us all not to try to leave town?''

"You like American Western movies, too," he said appreciatively. Then he sighed as if he bore the weight of the world on his shoulders. "But yes. That, miss, goes without saying—oh, here we are!''

The young maid had knocked softly and stepped just inside the door, holding out Carly's green velvet purse. "Thank you!" Carly said, stepping forward to accept her bag. She opened it. Her passport was still there, her wallet, her compact, atomizer, lipstick and traveler's checks. The letter was not in her purse.

She stared blankly at the inspector. "It isn't here.''

"Are you sure you had it with you?" Jon asked smoothly.

Carly stared at him but found it difficult to read anything in his golden wolf's eyes. Had he taken the letter? she wondered. He hadn't left the room.

But maybe he'd asked the maid to take it. No, he couldn't have done that, either. All of them had been present when he'd sent the maid out.

"I'm sure I had it with me," Carly insisted coolly.

Jon shrugged.

"Perhaps it was lost in the accident," the inspector suggested.

"Yes, perhaps," Carly murmured. She kept staring at Jon Vadim, who smiled in return.

"Well, I will certainly look into your sister's whereabouts," the inspector assured Carly. "And if anyone has information, I am available, and I will appreciate any assistance. Count—" the inspector clicked his heels together and inclined his head "—I will see myself out."

Jon Vadim nodded. The inspector left, and they all remained there, silent. Then Tanya leaped to her feet. "Damn! The band has quit playing."

"It's four a.m.," Geoffrey said. He made a grimace to Carly, who sat beside him on the rich leather sofa. "You throw quite a party, Jon."

"I'm going to bed," Tanya said. She stared around the room, almost as if she challenged them to stop her. Her cat eyes narrowed on Jon, but he wasn't even glancing her way. "A wonderful party!" she sniffed. "I wind up accused of murder!"

"I guess we're all accused of murder," Geoffrey said.

Jon waved a hand in the air dismissively. "No, it's just the inspector's way. Who knows? We are a dramatic people." He smiled at Carly. "This land was English when Henry II owned half of France and a dozen other properties. But we people are more French than anything else. We like passion and a sense of the theatrical. The inspector has to look everywhere. But someone from the village probably did bear the poor coachman a grudge."

Jon himself didn't believe what he was saying, Carly realized. His striking features were drawn into a pensive frown, and she was convinced that he thought that the inspector was right about one thing at least—the coachman had been killed to hurt the Vadims. Seeing the count there, distant, an air of casual command about him, Carly longed to go to him. Primeval instinct threatened to send her over to him to run her fingers over the planes of his face.

She was angry with him, too. She suspected him of somehow having stolen her letter. She wanted to know where her sister was and what he was hiding. She had to remember these things and resist his all-consuming magnetism.

"I need to get back to the hotel," Carly said.

"No!" Tanya protested. "You can't go back to the hotel. It's so late. You must stay here!"

"I'm sure that I'll be perfectly safe—"

"You will be safe," Jon said. "You'll stay right here."

Carly started to shake her head. She couldn't stay here. Being in the same...castle with him, even for a night, had to be dangerous. To her soul.

"I really can't stay," she insisted, "I don't have any of my things—"

"We have everything you might desire for the night," he said. "You must stay."

She wanted to protest just because he was so firmly denying her her wishes. But Geoffrey was up, taking her hand, patting it. "Carly, be reasonable. It's very late, and it's been a traumatic evening."

"Big damned deal!" Tanya said with exasperation. "Come on, and be a good little lamb. Let's get some sleep! I have plenty of things here for both of us."

Carly didn't appreciate the idea of being a "good little lamb," but she didn't want to be obnoxious.

"Carly, please," Jon insisted. "It would be best if you stayed." His amber eyes were upon her. She knew he was trying to be courteous, but it didn't sound as if he was *asking* her to stay. He was telling her.

"You can take the room right across from mine," Tanya told her, assuming it was all arranged. "I know it's been cleaned; the maids were in there this afternoon."

"Perfect," Jon Vadim agreed softly.

"Well, then..." Geoffrey kissed Carly's cheek. "We can talk tomorrow. I'm going to bed, too. Good night, Tanya, Alexi, Jon."

"I had best go home," Alexi said. He, too, kissed Carly's cheek, and then Tanya's. He winked at Carly. "I will be back."

"We wouldn't dream of forgetting to include you on any excursion," Tanya assured him sweetly. "Right, Jon?"

"Sure."

"Come on." Tanya tugged at Carly's hand. "I'll get you settled. Good night, all." Carly found herself looking back at Jon Vadim. There was a slight self-satisfied smile on his lips now. Their eyes met for a moment. Carly felt as if she should deny something, but he didn't say another word to her; he just watched her as she and Tanya left the library.

The castle was a large place, Carly thought as Tanya led her along. If Tanya weren't with her, she would be lost. Tanya must have been reading her mind, for she said, "It's not so bad. Just get your sense of direction from the mountains, and you'll know what you're doing. The terrace and the stairs are east. See?"

They came back to the terrace. The last of the guests was gone; everything was in disarray. "It will be all picked up by morning," Tanya murmured.

Carly saw the moon, which was still bright and full.

When they reached the stairway and then Tanya's room, she told Carly, "I'll just get you a toothbrush and toothpaste—oh, a nightgown. Then there's tomorrow. Is a denim dress okay?''

"Whatever," Carly said. "Thank you." She watched the beautiful "cat" as she moved around the room. Tanya was such a mass of contradictions. What was her part in all of this?

"Where did you meet Jon Vadim?" Carly asked casually.

"On the Riviera, several years ago," Tanya answered, then offered Carly a grimace. "I thought he was gorgeous at first. But he has a serious streak in him. I met a French wine baron at the same time, and the wine baron seemed the better deal."

"But you're still friends."

Tanya laughed. "Jon tolerates me. I have some money of my own, and I am interested in some of his charities. And he has some fascinating friends."

"Nothing romantic—between the two of you?"

"I thought there might be. But then . . ."

"But then what?"

Tanya looked at Carly and shook her head. "Nothing."

Carly tried to get her to speak, but Tanya refused to answer. "Nothing, honestly. It just isn't the right chemistry. And he's different lately, anyway. More serious than ever. And hard." She shivered. "He frowns so much now that he even looks different. But he is a good friend. And that inspector had no right giving him such a bad time. . . . Now, how's this? Do you have everything you might need?"

"Yes, everything," Carly said gratefully. "It's very nice of you to do this for me."

"It isn't anything at all." The other girl smiled. "Jasmine should have been here."

Carly paused. "You do know her, and you really aren't worried about her?"

Tanya shook her head. "You know your sister, too. You shouldn't be worried."

"Do you know why she left?"

Tanya shrugged. "Oh, I think she was mad at Jon. As I said, he's been different lately. Movement is one of Jasmine's fortes—if she was in a bad mood, running off to Paris would have been no big thing for her."

"Maybe," Carly murmured. "Anyway, thank you very much."

"Sure. Now, go to bed. Get some sleep. And please, lock your door, Carly."

"Are you afraid of something?"

"No! Honestly, I'm not. But that poor man was killed, so it would make sense to play it safe, right?"

Tanya led the way again, then opened the door across the hall. It was a beautiful room, but quite Gothic, Carly thought. It was huge, with a fireplace, a canopied bed, a writing desk, and plush chairs before the fire. There was a giant armoire in one corner, and the windows were covered in a soft gauze. "That door leads to the bath," Tanya advised her.

Carly was tired enough to crash headfirst into bed and stay there, but a bath sounded nice, too. The bathroom, which looked as though it had been installed sometime during the twenties or thirties, was beautiful. The big tub and porcelain sink were constructed in a Deco design. The floor was covered with tiny black and white tiles, against the back wall was a full-length mirror. Carly forgot that she was tired, cried out in delight, and started to run a bath.

"Well, I can see you're happy," Tanya said from the doorway. "Just don't forget—lock your door."

Carly nodded to her. "Thanks—very much, for everything. Good night."

Tanya left her. Carly found some bubble bath on a rack at the end of the tub and poured it into the bath, stripped and climbed in. She wrapped her hair above her head and lay back, letting the heat sink in as the bubbles covered her.

It had been one hell of a night, she decided. When she closed her eyes, she could still see Jon Vadim, tall and striking in his swirling black cape, his eyes eclipsing all else. She remembered how he'd held her, and she felt her blood heat up. It was insanity, she chided herself. She'd just met him. Yet maybe it was time she threw all caution to the wind. If her sister had no interest in the man, there was nothing to hold Carly back.

She started suddenly. She hadn't locked the bedroom door as Tanya had urged her to. She could swear that she heard someone out there now, in the bedroom.

She twisted around and stared at the bathroom door, a scream rising in her throat. The crystalline knob was turning....

"Tanya!" she called. "Is that you?"

Silence answered her cry. Carly leaped up, dripping and reaching for a towel. She ran to the door and threw it open. No one was there. She looked around the room. It seemed untouched. She closed her eyes, trying to recall. Had she put her sister's letter back into her purse when she'd been in the carriage? She was so certain she had. Had someone slipped upstairs earlier to steal the letter?

And had someone just been in her room, watching her, looking for... something?

"I'm losing my mind in this place!" she whispered.

She toweled herself dry, then slipped into the aquamarine nightgown and robe Tanya had given her. The set was satin, long and very sexy, with slits up one side of each garment. As she tied the belt, she met her own eyes in the mirror above the dresser. She was pale. Ridiculously pale.

And wide awake. It had to be five a.m. and she was desperately tired. But she would never sleep.

She decided to find the kitchen, or the bar. Hot cocoa or brandy or Scotch—she didn't care which one she found, as long as she could get her hands on something.

Carly left the room and quietly closed her door. She went down to the first floor. The terrace had already been cleaned. The moonlight was waning, and just a hint of the sun could be seen on the horizon. A sunrise here would be beautiful, she thought.

She entered the lower hallway, then discovered that she was hopelessly lost. She turned around to locate the sun. She was certain that Count Vadim would keep something in the library, which had been along the western hallway.

She was proud of herself when she found the right door and threw it open. But then a soft "Oh!" escaped her, for the library was not vacant. Jon Vadim, minus cape and costume, was sitting behind his desk. He was in an elegant smoking jacket, studying some papers. On the desk were a crystal decanter and a shot glass of the honey-colored liquid that filled the decanter.

"Carly," he said, standing, when he saw her. She almost backed away from the door. His gaze was warm, his rueful smile compelling.

"I—I couldn't sleep," she told him.

"Would you like some brandy?"

"Uh—no."

"Oh." He came around and leaned against the desk, idly folding his arms across his chest. "Then you're just prowling around the house?"

"No! Of—of course not."

"Then you were looking for a drink."

She sailed into the room, feeling like a fool. She wasn't afraid of him; it was just that things were just moving too quickly between them. He was very sophisticated. It wasn't that she was naive; he was just so arrogantly confident that she felt she needed to keep her distance. She was just too willing to fall for his charms, when there was every reason for her to mistrust him.

She circled the desk and found a second glass for the brandy upon a tray on a table nearby. She poured herself three fingers of brandy, willing her hands not to tremble, and made a soft sound of annoyance as she spilled a few drops upon the lace mat beneath the tray.

Jon Vadim approached, took the brandy from her fingers and set it down, and mopped up the mess with his handkerchief. "I would have been delighted to pour you a drink."

"Thank you."

She tried to smile, wanting to appear controlled and casual. "You're still up. You're up...very late."

He grinned at her wickedly. "Ah, but I'm a night person. Tell me, Carly. Are you usually up so late?"

"Until morning? No, I'm not."

"But you're adaptable." It was a statement, not a question. The count drew his own conclusions, she saw.

"Adaptable. But not easily led." She spoke with assurance, though she felt very little of it. At that moment, she thought, she would probably follow him anywhere.

"Common sense is a great virtue," he said.

Yes, and she usually had lots of it, she thought. What was happening to her here, she didn't know. He was laughing at her, she realized, but it seemed to be a tender laughter. She smiled. "Yes, it is a great virtue."

"But not much fun." He lifted his glass to hers, stepping in front of her. "Cheers."

"Cheers."

She swallowed the brandy. Her heart was beating a thousand times a minute. She was certain he could see the pulse that raged against her throat. What was this? she wondered in a moment's panic. This hypnotic man could steal souls. She wanted to run, and she wanted to fall into his arms.

"Well..." She smiled, setting down her glass. "I think I could probably sleep now."

From somewhere far away she heard the baying of a dog. Then, too, came the haunting sad, slow strains of a violin playing a waltz.

"How lovely," she murmured, staring into his eyes.

He nodded. "It is beautiful." He put down his glass and reached for her fingers. "We were interrupted this evening. We never finished our dance."

"What?..." Carly whispered in protest. He smiled, took her hand and swiftly led her out of the library. Within moments they were on the terrace. The dying moon was a white orb in the sky, and the muted, misty colors of a new morning fell gently upon them. As if on cue, the dog ceased to howl, and the strains of the distant violin hauntingly floated on the morning air.

Jon bowed low to her, then caught both her hands and swept her into his arms. He held her tightly against him and swirled her around the room as if they danced on clouds.

She looked into his eyes, thinking that the tenderness and fascination she found there could not be a lie. This night was magic—sweet, rough magic. His hand upon her back felt like a brand on her satiny robe. There was so little between them, she thought. She felt the hardness of his chest against her breasts. She felt his hips and the muscles of his thighs and sensed a rich warmth seeping into her, filling her heart. She couldn't draw her eyes from the amber depths of his.

Suddenly they weren't dancing anymore, though they were still touching, her breasts against his chest, hip to hip, legs almost entwined. He cupped her chin with one hand and slowly brought his mouth down upon hers. When she felt the sweet, keen pressure of his lips, she parted hers. The pulse of her heart raced so swiftly that it was agonizing. She gripped his shoulders and played her fingers over his back. She flicked at his lips with her tongue, then fell back into the greedy depths of the kiss again. She felt his hands upon her in a questing touch. With his palms he teased her nipples, then curled his hands around her breasts to explore their fullness. She ached at his touch. New fever rippled through her. The need, the hunger, filled her breasts, then pulsed through her veins to the core of her and erupted like fire in the pit of her abdomen. She wanted to fall against him and let the satin material slide off her to the floor. She wanted to feel his touch more thoroughly, wanted to drown forever in the magic of the kiss.

Jon Vadim wondered at the magic, too, of this night, this woman. He didn't think he'd ever seen anyone quite like her. Her skin was as soft as her satin gown, and as he held her he felt his pulse race, his muscles constrict. From the moment he'd seen her, standing like a lost princess among the wreckage of the carriage, he'd felt a curious ache seep into him. It was a hunger, deep and fervent, like nothing he'd ever felt. He wanted her; at this moment he burned for her. But he knew she would not be easily taken, nor would the hunger be easily appeased.

He wished to God he could tell her the truth. No, he just wished that he could sweep her off the terrace and up into the privacy of his room.

Already, though, he felt her drawing away. Just as the night sky was losing the magic of the moon, he was losing the sweet moment of her trust.

And it was just as well, perhaps, he decided. It was all a lie.

Carly met the question in his eyes with a shake of her head.

"There is something here," he said softly. "I really don't think you can fight it. I don't think I can fight it."

"I—I want to know where Jasmine is," Carly said. "I want to know what is going on here."

"Jasmine is safe. I swear it!" he told her.

"I want to trust you."

"Then trust me."

She had to get away from him. She wanted to hold him again, to feel his touch, and he knew it. There *was* something there, some rough magic on the mist and in the breeze. And for the life of her, she couldn't deny it or fight it.

She shook her head again, turned away from him and hurried back along the terrace.

The moon had disappeared. The sun was rising, golden and glowing.

She didn't look back. If she had, she knew, she would see that he hadn't moved. He had stayed there and watched her run.

She fled up the stairs as if chased by demons. This time she did lock the door, once she'd entered the room. She slipped off the robe, ran to the bed and slid beneath the covers. She pulled them up to her chest and lay back, breathing hard.

She glanced toward the door, then smiled at herself. She was being a fool. She knew he hadn't followed her. She thought again about the legends of the region.

If the count wanted to reach her, no lock in the world could keep him from doing so.

She almost laughed aloud. One night, and he was all that filled her thoughts. Her heart still beat too rapidly. She had to take care. He was too fascinating. Too powerful, too masculine. And she was being drawn in way too quickly for a woman with good sense.

Hearing footsteps in the hallway, Carly tensed suddenly.

She held her breath.

The inspector had said that whoever had killed the coachman might have wanted to kill her. Perhaps the footsteps moving so stealthily in the hall were those of a killer, coming for her....

She prayed in a whisper and shot out of bed. On her bare feet she hurried across the room, barely breathing as she listened.

She exhaled, slumping against the wall. The footsteps were not coming any closer. They had stopped at Tanya's door across the hall. And no one was breaking in on Tanya. Carly heard a soft rap, Tanya's door was opened. Tanya's voice. "There you are." Tanya giggled. "Come in, love."

A masculine whisper made a reply.

The door was closed. There was silence out in the hallway, then Carly heard a soft moan and a whimper.

Carly felt her cheeks flame. Tanya was meeting a lover, and Carly was spying on her. She had no right....

But she did have a right; she just didn't want Tanya's lover to be Jon Vadim. Tanya had denied any relationship but hinted at something else.

Jasmine... But Jon Vadim had denied a relationship with her sister. It was all so confusing. She was worried silly and was falling beneath a spell, despite it all. A man was dead, she had nearly been killed herself, and all that mattered was Jon Vadim.

She swore out loud and vowed to herself that she would get to the bottom of things.

She walked back to the bed and crawled into it once more. She tried to sleep, but to her horror she kept wondering about the pair behind the other door. At last she pounded her pillow and crashed against it, determined to go to sleep.

She slept at last. But her sleep was filled with dreams. She kept seeing Jon Vadim. He walked to her through fields of mist, smiling at her, and though she knew she should be afraid, she stood still and waited.

He kissed her, and she felt that the clothing covering them both melted into the mist. They lay down together in clouds. He kissed her, the mist swirling around them. Then he rose above her, she saw only his golden glowing eyes and heard laughter, then Jasmine's warning voice.

"He'll steal your soul.... He'll steal your soul...."

Carly knew it but could not stop him. He came to her again, and she stretched out her arms to receive him.

Carly had no idea what time it was when she awoke. For a long while she remained on the bed, wondering what of the preceding day had been real and what had been imagined.

She groaned as she rose. She still felt so sleepy. She glanced at her watch and saw that it was almost three in the afternoon.

Another bath might help, she decided.

In the tub she mused that she must be losing her mind. She was in Transylvania, so she was creating imaginary demons. She was exhausted, which was why she had nightmares and woke up with a splitting headache. She closed her eyes but trembled even as she did so. Jon Vadim was real. So were her feelings for him. He was devastating, and she was not immune.

"But not stupid, either!" she assured herself. The hot water felt so good. It eased all the tension from her. With the count she would be very strong and somewhat caustic. She wasn't going to fall like putty into his arms anymore.

"Carly."

Her eyes flew open. She faced the mirrored wall, and that was where she saw him first, in the mirror.

He was in black jeans and a black polo shirt. His hair was damp and fell in a wave over his forehead. Where the V of the sweater lay against his chest, little tufts of hair showed, giving him a raw, sexual appeal.

Her eyes met his in the mirror.

At least he had a mirror image, she told herself. Unlike a vampire.

But she couldn't pull her gaze away. She noticed the pulse beating against his throat and saw his features tense. He stood still, but she could feel the vibrant energy within him.

And the hunger.

And she herself felt it sweeping through her body like a storm, making her weak, making her tremble. Something terribly strong leaped between them. She felt him...with all of her naked flesh, with the length of her body. She had never known what it was like to want a man so.

"What are you doing in here?" she demanded.

"You didn't answer the maid's knock on your door. You didn't answer my knock. I was worried."

"You didn't knock," she reproached him.

"I did knock. You didn't hear me."

Her throat was dry. She wanted to offer him total indignation, but could barely whisper. "You shouldn't be here."

"I had to see that you were all right."

"I'm fine."

"Yes, I see that."

You should go now! she wanted to yell, but didn't say it out loud. She said it with her eyes.

He didn't speak out loud, either. Nor did he leave. He continued to watch her, and powerless, she watched him.

She searched desperately for the common sense she was so proud of having. He was in the bathroom, uninvited, while she lay in the tub, ridiculously vulnerable.

She wanted to whirl around to face him. She wanted to accost him, to rail against him. She couldn't seem to move.

He entered the bathroom. Their eyes continued to meet in the mirror as he knelt behind her, as he drew his thumb gently down her cheek.

Then he tilted her chin. Their gazes met now without the aid of the mirror. He kissed her. Lightly at first, then more deeply.

He slipped his arms into the water, cupping her breasts with his hands. He moved his thumbs over her nipples, his fingers splayed over her flesh.

Heedless of the bubbles, he pulled her into his arms and lifted her, dripping, against him. Then he carried her into the bedroom.

Carly stared up at him. She knew she should say something, stop him, but she couldn't speak.

He laid her down and stretched himself beside her. She felt his eyes rake over her, taking in all of her. Then he kissed her again, and she felt the ragged fever of his breath, felt the fire of his touch. He kissed her lips, her throat. He ran his hand from her breast to the curve of her hip. Flaming liquid seemed to skim along her flesh as he stroked from her abdomen to her thigh.

Then his kiss fell to her breast and she felt a sweet explosion of pure desire fill her as he closed his mouth over her nipple and delicately played his teeth against it. She dug her fingers into his hair and tossed and turned in an agony of longing. She arched against his touch as she whispered, "No, please... It's too... fast."

He fell dead still against her. For an eternity he held her. She felt her heart thunder against his, felt the terrible constriction of his muscles.

She wanted him so badly. He must hate her, should probably ignore her, because she should have denied him from the start. She should have railed against him for entering her room, and she should have been indignant....

She shouldn't even be here.

But she was, lying naked beside him, denying him, wanting him. She had never felt such an awful confusion.

He moved at last. Softly he kissed the valley between her breasts, then he rose above her. He studied her without condemnation.

She shook her head. "I'm sorry," she murmured. With a soft cry she reached up and locked her arms around him, burying her head against his neck. She started to shiver, cold and wet where her body wasn't touched by his.

Then she realized that she had turned him away, but was holding him again. She released him, twisting out of his hold. She leaped from the bed and rushed into the bath, where she wrapped a towel around herself. When she returned to the bedroom, he was gone.

Chapter 4

Carly lay in bed for a long while. Though she sensed that he understood, she still felt that she needed to explain. What could she say to the man? *Yes, I'm dying to touch you, too. It's just that it's all....*

So sudden, so fast. At this time yesterday she hadn't even known him. But she couldn't pretend there wasn't some sweet chemistry between them.

She hadn't handled things very well, she knew. She had let it all escalate—and then she had said no, like a confused teenager in the back seat of a car.

At last she rose. Glancing out the windows, she saw that it was already growing dark. She had lost the day. This seemed to be a place where night reigned supreme anyway, she thought dryly. Night hid secrets, and it could also hide the truth.

She dressed in clothing borrowed from Tanya. What was Tanya up to this evening? she wondered. And who had Tanya's nocturnal visitor been?

Secrets, she mused. The place was awash with them. And the main one was still where Jasmine was—hiding?

Carly brushed her hair, then paused, staring at her image. She had to believe in Jon Vadim. She didn't think he'd gone out and killed the coachman, and she was certain he hadn't done away with her sister, either. She didn't know why she should believe in him. She shouldn't believe in him, really. But she did. Such things didn't always make sense, or else they were part of one's sixth sense.

She turned, sighing. She had to say something to him.

She left her room and went down the stairway and through the terrace. A young girl was sweeping the floor. Carly smiled at her, and the girl smiled back shyly. How many people worked in the castle? Carly wondered. None of them seemed alarmed about the recent events. If they suspected Jon Vadim of maniacal behavior, wouldn't they all be running for their lives?

She smiled at the image and approached the library. The door was closed, and she paused. She should knock, she thought. But as she stood there she realized that she wanted to run back to her room. Squaring her shoulders, she told herself that chances didn't come that often in life. Magic was fragile and ethereal and not at all easy to touch.

She couldn't just walk away.

She knocked on the door and turned the old brass knob at the same time. She stepped into the room and felt her heart begin a double-time beat. He was there.

He was seated behind his desk, studying some document. She didn't speak. Now that she had made it into the room, she couldn't think of what she wanted to say.

Jon Vadim looked up. He didn't smile, and she wondered if he was still angry. He had a right to be, she thought.

"Ms. Kiernan," he murmured.

He had no right to be so proper, she decided. His British accent made it worse. He sounded remote and distant and arrogantly aloof.

"What is it?" he asked, and she realized that she was staring at him and hadn't moved. He rose, came around the desk and sat on the edge, watching her with great care.

She shook her head. "I just wanted to say that I was sorry."

"For what?"

Even if it had all meant nothing to him, he owed her more than that, she thought. "Nothing! Never mind!" She whirled around to leave; the whole thing had been ridiculous.

"Wait! Please wait!" He caught her shoulders and turned her around. His hair was brushed back, she saw. He seemed a little older than she remembered.

"Please, tell me," he said. "Why are you sorry?"

The question seemed sincere. If it was sincere, she thought, things were worse than she had imagined. She pulled away from him, backing toward the door.

"Count, I am aware that you spend a great deal of your time in Monte Carlo, playing the roulette wheel, and in the Caribbean, yachting about. It's a different life-style. From mine, that is. But I come from the big city, and even there, people behave with some thought and some purpose!"

He inclined his head in confusion and crossed his arms over his chest, smiling down at her like a patient parent. "I really don't know what you're trying to say."

She didn't know either, except that she had just made a fool of herself. "Just now, in my room. What you did...what I said—oh, never mind. I'm leaving. Thank you very much for an...interesting evening. If Jasmine should contact you, let her know that I'm very worried, please!"

"Carly—"

She didn't wait to hear any more but slammed her way out of the library. She raced through the terrace, her face flaming. How could he have behaved so coldly! she wondered. Had he forgotten the moments in the hunter's cottage, or the way that they had danced? Had he forgotten the way he had touched her in her room not an hour earlier?

She ran up the stairs, determined to leave Castle Vadim as quickly as possible. She shouldn't have stayed last night. On the landing she nearly collided with the young maid who had been on the terrace earlier.

"Madame, excusez-moi, s'il vous plaît!"

Carly managed to smile. "No. It was my fault, excuse me, *s'il vous plaît*. Please, tell me, what is your name?"

"Marie."

"Marie. Where is the nearest telephone?"

"Oh." Marie smiled with relief. "*Ici*. Here, in the hallway, madame." They passed majestic windows that looked out on the courtyard below. Halfway along the hall, Marie paused. There was a great Deco-style niche in the wall, and within it was a small marble bench with a matching table and an elegant brass telephone. Carly thanked Marie and sat down. She stared at the telephone and realized that there was no way to dial.

"Marie!"

She looked out to the hallway, but the maid was already gone. Carly picked up the receiver and heard a dial tone. She jiggled the phone and an operator responded. Carly tried to remember some simple French, but her mind was blank. "*Taxi, s'il vous plaît.* I'm at Castle Vadim," she said at last.

The operator returned her words quickly spoken in French. In frustration Carly repeated the word "taxi," then the woman impatiently said, "*Ùn moment, s'il vous plaît!*"

The line went dead. Sighing, Carly hung up. She'd have to try to find Tanya. Tanya had been involved with a Frenchman and must remember something of the language!

Carly walked idly over to the windows.

Jon was down in the courtyard, standing by Satan. He was all in black again—black jeans, high black boots—and it looked as if he had been riding.

He sure moved fast, Carly thought bitterly. And then, despite herself, she felt a warmth sweep through her, and heady palpitations seized her heart. He looked up, directly at her. With the amber eyes of the wolf he stared up into her features and offered her a dazzling smile. He waved, still grinning. His appearance, tall and unconquerable beside the prancing midnight stallion, was totally arresting. I could fall in love with him so easily, Carly thought.

She stepped back, frightened. She thought of all the times she'd gone to dinner or the theater or skating with an eligible man, the proper type for her: a stockbroker, a banker, a research assistant at the Natural History Museum. She'd always tried to laugh and enjoy herself. No matter how hard she'd wanted to, she just hadn't been able to feel anything for them other than friendship, other than a polite interest....

And now here was Jon Vadim. When she should be only politely interested, when she should protect her feelings with steel gates, she was as lost as an innocent young girl, and far too pliable.

She looked out the window again. Jon Vadim was gone.

Carly started as the phone rang. Maybe the operator had understood her, after all, and was calling to say that a taxi was on its way.

Carly started for the phone. She sat down on the marble bench and picked up the receiver. Someone had already answered the phone—Jon Vadim. He was speaking with a woman, quickly, firmly, and mentioned "taxi." The woman murmured, *"D'accord,"* and the phone clicked off.

"Wait!" Carly cried.

"I'll be right there," Jon said to her.

"No! That's not what—"

The phone went dead. Frustrated, Carly replaced the receiver. She looked up—and nearly screamed.

He was already there, standing before her in his black outfit, looking entirely prepossessing. Carly stood to face him.

"You had no right to do that!" she told him.

His eyes narrowed. "To do what?" he asked carefully.

"You sent the taxi away, didn't you?" She was certain he had, but couldn't begin to imagine why. He'd behaved so coldly in the library that she would have thought that he'd be pleased to get rid of her.

"I, uh, yes, I sent the taxi away."

"Why?"

"Why?" he repeated.

"Why, damn you! I want to leave here and go back to the hotel. You must know that!"

"But you can't leave," he said.

"I can, and I intend to."

He shook his head. "You mustn't."

He took a step closer to her, and she was caught in the little Deco alcove against the wall and the marble bench. His after-shave drifted around her like a mesmerizing mist, and she wondered why she hadn't smelled it in the library. She didn't ponder on it long, however, for he flattened his palms against the wall, imprisoning her, and he smiled. She stiffened, trying to prepare her defenses.

"Please, don't go," he murmured.

"I can't stay here."

"I can't let you go. There's too much between us. I can give you time—all the time in the world. But I can't let you go."

"Very nice. Lovely. Two minutes ago I wasn't terribly sure that you remembered my name," she remarked dryly.

"Two minutes ago?"

"In the library."

"Oh, yes, in the library." He stared at her, waiting.

Carly pushed against his chest and slipped beneath his arms. "Damn you, stop this! I can't play this game."

Something dark and dangerous fell over his eyes. He caught her arm and dragged her back. "I'm not playing any games! I'm trying to be as adult and courteous as I can be under the circumstances."

"Under the circumstances!"

"Well, Ms. Kiernan, you do run hot and cold."

"I do!"

"I would say that I needed to call upon a certain restraint, patience, tolerance, and self-control."

"Why, you conceited!—" Carly snapped, incredulous. First he'd behaved as if nothing had happened—
and now this!

"You had no right being in there! You caused the
entire situation. Now, I'm trying—with a great deal of
restraint, patience, courtesy and tolerance—to see that
the situation does not recur! Now, if you won't let me
phone a taxi, I'll walk back to the damned village!"

She tried to jerk free from his grasp; he held her still.
Her knees felt weak, and a wave of trembling and panic
washed over her. Was he all that he seemed? He had
appeared in the darkness on his black horse. A wolf had
run from his simple, quiet words. With his arms encir-
cling her, she knew that he had the strength to do
whatever he would—hold her there indefinitely; wind
his fingers around her neck and strangle her. She should
be afraid.

But she wasn't. Not that he would harm her, anyway. She still couldn't begin to understand why, but she
wasn't afraid that he would hurt her.

What she was afraid of was that she would forget the
fight, forget how foolish he had already made her feel.
And she was most afraid that he would touch her again
in such a way that all she would want was more of him,
more of his touch.

"Jon..." she whispered in protest. He eased his hold
on her. He clenched his teeth and let her go.

"I will walk," she stated.

"It's fifteen miles, and you aren't walking anywhere."

"Really?" Arching a brow, she spun around and hurried toward her room. All she needed was her purse. She would send for her gown and have Tanya's dress cleaned before she returned it.

When she reached her room, she heard him call her name. She opened the door, and he was suddenly behind her, pulling her into the room. Then he was holding her arms and staring down at her, and his eyes were full of heat and tension and sincerity.

"I don't want you to leave here." He paused, then added softly, "Not unless you're going home."

"Oh, no. I'm not going home. Before I leave this place, I want to know where my sister is!"

"Then you must stay here."

"I don't have to—"

"Please."

"Why is it that you are able to manipulate people so! Damn it! You order me about, then you suddenly sound so courteous, and I feel like a churlish brat!"

She noticed that a smile tugged at his lips. He cupped her chin, stroking her cheek with his thumb, and said, "Because I really don't want you to leave."

"You are sending me insane!" Carly protested, pulling away from his touch. He could make her give in too easily, she knew, if his hands were upon her. As she stared at him she realized that he seemed younger again. It was the smile, the laughter, she decided. They swept away years.

"Carly, come here." He beckoned her gently.

She shook her head but walked back toward him, anyway. He embraced her, and despite herself, she curled her own arms around his neck.

"I swear to you," he told her, "to the very best of my knowledge Jasmine is in Paris. She is alive and well—

and being Jasmine. And I swear to you, too...that I just can't let you go. If you're going to stay, stay here."

"If I mean so much to you, Jon, why are you so anxious for me to go home?"

He shrugged, then threaded his fingers through her hair, watching as the soft strands fell back to her shoulders. "The coachman was killed," he stated.

"Someone is killed somewhere every day. Even in the most remote and crime-free places. New York has its fair share of criminals," Carly said, searching his face.

But his amber eyes gave away nothing. He shrugged again, and his rueful smile deepened. "Maybe I am worried. Maybe it is true—the villagers aren't murdered every day around here."

"Then you suspect—"

"I don't suspect anything. I'll just make a deal with you. You stay here, or you go home."

"What?"

"Please, Carly."

"I wish I understood."

"I wish that you would believe in me."

"I..." she began.

"What?"

"I do believe in you," she breathed.

She'd done it again, she realized. Her fears were all well-founded, for she had earnestly meant to leave, and here she was, surrendering to his command. It was a command, she knew. No matter how endearingly phrased it was.

He pulled her close and just held her. She heard the beating of his heart and her own. Feeling the strength and the warmth of his caress, she buried her head against his chest, glad to be held. She wanted to imagine that there was no future and no past and no secrets or confusions between them. Just for a matter of moments she would like to feel loved again, loved and cherished. And she would like to give way to the rich and heady excitement that filled her and sizzled and seared, deep inside....

He drew away. She was dazzled by his dark good looks and rueful smile. "I have your things."

"Pardon me?"

"I have your things. I went to the hotel and brought back your things."

"But—" she started to say.

"I'll send someone up with them right away." He kissed her forehead, caressing the nape of her neck with his thumb and forefinger. Then he pulled away. "Slowly," he told her. "I'll have to learn to keep my hands off you. It isn't easy, you know. It's worse...now. I can dream in living color."

She flushed, aware that he was referring to the moments they had spent together on the bed. His eyes and words reminded her that he knew her now, from head to toe, and she grew warm again with that knowledge.

"I don't have color," she quipped lightly.

"We can rectify that."

"Now? Aren't—" She paused a little breathlessly. "We must be late for dinner by now."

He laughed. "Any excuse, hmm? But yes. Dinner is on the terrace at eight o'clock." He glanced at his watch. "One hour. I'll come for you."

"I can find my way—"

"I'll come for you." With the white flash of a smile, he left her. Carly sank onto her bed and tried to go over everything that had happened. She'd been furious; she should have been gone by now.

But in an hour he was going to come back to take her down to dinner.

There was a knock on her door.

"Come in!" Carly called.

It was one of the grooms, a handsome boy of about eighteen. He was carrying Carly's luggage. He set it down and she thanked him, and he nodded to her with pleasure.

When the door closed, Carly reflected that everyone who worked for the count seemed happy here. Maybe they made good money here, she thought dryly. But people could make good money and still hate their jobs, she mused.

She should have been gone—back to the hotel.

But she was here, and he was going to come for her in an hour.

Despite herself, Carly leaped to her feet and set her suitcase on the bed. She was anxious to look her best.

At five of eight he was back.

It seemed that dinner at the castle was always a dress affair. Jon Vadim was in a tux, which he wore with a noble flair. The black of his outfit complemented the darkness of his hair and contrasted with the extraordinary amber of his eyes. He looked at her with a twinkle of humor in his eyes, and Carly knew from the time he bowed and politely took her arm to escort her that he was well aware of his effect upon her.

"You're beautiful," he told her.

"Thank you."

She had chosen an off-the-shoulder gown with a bouffant skirt in Chinese silk.

"Your own design?"

"Yes."

"I'm heartbroken. You dressed for Geoffrey and not for me."

Carly was glad her eyes were lowered. She'd forgotten all about Geoffrey—and the fact that she had expressed a desire to work with the man. Jon Vadim had that kind of power; he made her forget everything else.

"I didn't dress for anyone," she lied, meeting his eyes. She lowered her gaze again; he knew.

He led her toward the stairs and held her hand as they walked down.

"You really are conceited," she told him as they reached the landing. "And ridiculously arrogant."

"I am not. I'm anxious and frightened and terrified."

"Of what?"

"That I'll lose you."

"You don't have me, so you can't lose me. And I don't appreciate your making light of this."

"I'm not making light of anything. I'm trying very hard to keep my distance, that's all," he said.

They'd reached the terrace. Carly couldn't reply. Tanya was there, looking beautiful in a long, slinky gown with a thigh-high slash. Geoffrey was by her side, head lowered. He appeared very different without his mummy wrappings, Carly mused. He was an attractive man, tall and lean, with a craggy, endearing face. She didn't realize she was staring until he laughed.

"So you prefer the costume, huh?" he said, eyebrow raised.

"No! Oh, no, I'm so sorry. You just gave me a start!"

He laughed, and Tanya came over and told her that her dress was stunning. "You should be making a mint, doll."

"Don't turn her head," Geoffrey said. "Not until she's done my show."

"You really want me to?" Carly asked.

"Of course."

"See, Carly? Something good has come of being here," Jon said. He stared at her and smiled, and she wondered if he was being cynical or if he was really pointing out the benefits of her stay.

"Where's Alexi?" she asked.

"Here I am." Alexi stepped onto the terrace with a drink. "I was in the bar. Can I go fix something for you two?"

Jon waved a hand. "I'll get our drinks. Carly, what would you like?"

She started to say that she didn't want anything, then decided that she very much wanted a drink, and she asked him for a Rusty Nail. He smiled—another mocking smile, she thought—and left them. She commented how pretty the set table looked.

Alexi nodded vaguely. "Yes, the count does live elegantly."

"I'm sure your home is every bit as elegant," Carly suggested.

Alexi laughed. "No, no, *chérie*, it is not. But—" he shuddered dramatically "—though my home is not so elegant, it is warm and nice. And I'd rather enjoy my genteel poverty without the Vadim curse than all the Vadim riches in the world."

"The Vadim curse?" Carly asked with a laugh.

"Of course!" Geoffrey broke in.

"Madness!" Tanya said teasingly.

"Oh, come now!" Carly scoffed.

Geoffrey laughed. "There's only a skeleton or two in the closets here."

"Right. The majority of them are in the basement," Tanya said.

"Laugh if you will," Alexi said. "They've been known to howl at the moon."

"Telling tales again, Alexi?"

Jon returned, and Carly started guiltily. He walked back onto the terrace, smiling at Alexi, and handed Carly her drink.

"We're trying to infuse some mood here," Tanya said lightly.

"Of course." Smiling at Carly, Jon took her arm and led her around the table. "We're as rampantly mad as can be, as frightening as a cave of vampire bats. Born that way, of course."

He was joking—of course, Carly thought. But she sensed a certain bitterness behind the words and wondered what was true about the Vadim family and what was not.

She believed in Jon, she reminded herself. She was here because she believed in him. But she couldn't help the strange thoughts that plagued her mind. She found it difficult to understand Jon's behavior.

She was seated between Jon and Geoffrey as the meal was served by the butler and Marie and another maid. It *was* all very elegant, and Carly wondered idly what it was like to live this way all the time. Jasmine was probably accustomed to such service, since she moved among a moneyed crowd. Carly wasn't sure she herself would really like it. The castle seemed to lack a certain intimacy.

When she caught Jon watching her with a speculative smile, she wondered if he was reading her mind. She flushed, sipped her wine and looked away.

Geoffrey monopolized her attention for the rest of the meal. They ate delicious lamb, some of the best Carly had ever had. And the wine was wonderful. As she listened to Geoffrey's enthusiastic plans for his next production, she ate and drank too much, and when the meal was over, she felt warm and languid and very comfortable. Jon came in on the conversation, comparing the theater in London with that in New York. He talked about a particular production at the Drury Lane that was similar to the one Geoffrey had in mind. Carly didn't have much to contribute, so she leaned back to listen. It was nice to feel relaxed and at ease—and normal!—here, she mused.

She closed her eyes and realized that Alexi and Tanya were deeply engrossed in conversation, in French. Alexi seemed angry, and Tanya sounded bored. Carly wished she could understand what they were saying. She glanced at Jon and at Geoffrey, but neither was paying any attention. Geoffrey was creating a stage out of his knife and dessert fork, and Jon was quick to show the angle of the sets with an arrangement of after-dinner mints.

But then Tanya yawned, long and expressively, and they were all forced to notice her. She made a display of studying her slim gold watch. "It's after midnight. Do you believe that?"

"Easily," Geoffrey said. "We didn't go to bed until this morning."

Carly found herself yawning, too.

Geoffrey laughed. "Yawning is contagious, you know."

"I suppose," Carly agreed, and stood. Geoffrey, Alexi and Jon were instantly on their feet, too. There was something nice about the old-world atmosphere

here, she realized. It was the wine. She'd had a great deal of it, and bed would definitely be the best place for her.

"I agree with Tanya," she murmured a little apologetically. "I'm sorry. I think I'm exhausted."

"Geoffrey, you bored her to exhaustion!" Alexi said.

"Geoffrey, you did no such thing," Carly insisted.

"I'll walk you up," Jon offered.

"No!" She was aware that she'd spoken too quickly, and bit her inner lip as everyone looked at her with discreet half smiles. "Please, Jon, Geoffrey, Alexi—all of you, stay here. Tanya and I can go up together."

"Perfect." Tanya too, rose. She took Alexi's hands and let him kiss both her cheeks. "Good night. And Geoff…" On tiptoe, she kissed his lips lightly, then did the same with Jon.

Carly stepped back before she could become embroiled in it all. "Good night, Alexi, it was wonderful seeing you again."

"You'll not get rid of me," he promised. "You see, I made it back for dinner this evening. And I think I'll stay the night."

"You're welcome, of course," Jon told him. Carly wondered whether or not he meant it. Then she didn't care. She was really exhausted and wanted only to escape Jon, though she didn't have the strength or the will to fight him at the moment.

"Bonne nuit," Jon said softly.

Smiling weakly, she turned from his gaze and hurried after Tanya.

"He definitely has his eye on you," Tanya remarked as they walked up the stairs. "Ouch." She paused to slip her high-heel sandals off. She grimaced at Carly. "One just doesn't wear sneakers to dinner here."

Carly laughed. "No, I suppose not."

"I wouldn't have minded being mistress of this place," Tanya said with a sigh.

"But—"

"There is nothing between us," Tanya assured her with a laugh. "For a while I thought that Jas—" She broke off.

"Jasmine," Carly said.

Tanya shook her head. "No, no—"

"Then what were you saying?"

"Honest, I don't remember what I was about to say." She leaped up the remaining steps in her stocking feet. "I'm so tired! We should have a day tomorrow to do something with. Some sight-seeing. It's a beautiful country, the best of western Europe and the best of eastern Europe. Good night!" She disappeared through the door to her room.

Carly entered her own room. Her suitcases had been emptied. She hurried over to the armoire and saw that it had been filled with her things.

Marie had probably come in to unpack for her, she decided. But still, it bothered her. She reflected again on the letter from Jasmine that had disappeared. Someone, she was certain, had gone through her purse.

She was too tired to deal with it at that moment, though. She had meant to leave today but hadn't, putting her faith instead in an arrogant, mysterious and confusing man. She was here for another night, at least.

Carly shed her gown, kicked off her evening slippers and rolled down her stockings. In the armoire she found her own flannel nightgown, which was nowhere near as sexy or as elegant as the one she had worn the night before. Evidence of a life-style, she thought wryly. Tanya's was definitely more exciting—and attractive—than hers.

She was considering changing that, she thought as she lay down. Just hours before, she had lain here with Jon, and they had almost...

She thumped her pillow and wiggled down into it. It had been so long, but she knew he would make things easy. All the same, her emotions would run deep, and she would need more than just expertise from him; she would need to believe that the magic was real.

She was too nervous and excited to sleep. But she was exhausted, too. She closed her eyes, which felt so very heavy....

She dreamed she was not alone. Someone was with her, watching over her. Someone who tenderly touched her cheek, then bent down and very gently kissed her lips. The touch was just a whisper of breath, barely a touch at all. Sweet and provocative. She wanted to reach for more....

Carly awoke with a start, certain someone really was in the room with her. It was the dream, she told herself. But it wasn't. She was tense and frightened because the danger was real.

She didn't move.

No one could be in the room, she assured herself. She had made sure to lock the door that night, and from the moonlight filtering into the room she could see that the door was still closed.

But she could feel someone... or something!

She turned her head carefully, looking toward the balcony and toward the rear of the room. There was very little light, and she couldn't tell what she was seeing. Shadow and substance converged. First there was a form in the room, and then there was nothing at all.

She closed her eyes and opened them again. Nothing was there.

Shaking, she sat up, turned on the bedside lamp and wrapped her arms about herself.

She was alone.

For several seconds she just sat there. Then she jumped up and checked the door. It was bolted.

She walked over to the French doors. They too were locked. She opened them, and the night breeze rushed in upon her. Up in the sky was a gibbous moon, which was still nearly full.

Carly heard the sudden, startling howl of a wolf.

She peered across the courtyard. The wolf was there, looking toward her window. It was a big wolf. She thought she could see the creature's eyes. They were golden in the darkness, golden beneath the moon.

It howled again, seeming to watch her, then it turned and raced off, a wraith in the night.

Carly shivered. "There was no wolf in this room!" she whispered. Then she added in confusion, "There was nothing in this room. Nothing at all!"

She came back in and locked the French doors. She checked the door to the hall again. It was still firmly bolted.

Leaving the light on, Carly crawled back into bed and pulled the covers to her neck.

Eventually she closed her eyes again and dozed. She had vivid, though sketchy, dreams. A wolf was running after her, a wolf with golden eyes. He would run on all fours. . . .

And then he would run on two legs. He was no longer a wolf, but a man. A man with golden, amber-glowing eyes. A man in a flowing black cape.

A man who bent down to seal her lips with a kiss and steal her breath and her very soul.

Chapter 5

In the morning Marie brought Carly a breakfast tray. In broken English she told Carly that the count would like her downstairs by ten; a drive through the estate and the nearby countryside had been planned. There would be seven excursions altogether.

Geoffrey, Alexi and Tanya were with Carly and the count as they rode over the estate. Jon, on Satan, kept a discreet distance from Carly. Sometimes she would catch him watching her, however, and it was almost as if he were asking with vast amusement whether this wasn't just what she wanted. Tanya was an excellent horsewoman, and Geoffrey and Alexi were very comfortable, too. Carly was grateful for the trail riding she had done through Central Park, so she didn't feel like a complete idiot. Still, when the day was over, after they'd traveled through the internationally famous vineyards and over the fields and farmland, she was in some pain and had difficulty pretending that she could walk normally. Sitting through dinner was a nightmare, and she escaped as soon as the meal was finished.

The second day, the five rode again through the countryside. They passed flocks of sheep and charming little houses where the storks nested in the chimneys. They stopped for a picnic and drank wine, and for a while Carly let her guard down. She laughed and ate grapes with the others while she rested her head on Jon Vadim's lap and occasionally looked up into his magic gaze.

The third day, they all went into the village. The houses were exquisite cottages that might have jumped right out of *Hansel and Gretel*. They lunched in the one major restaurant, where people scurried to serve them, happy to please the count.

They explored the shops and meandered through the quaint alleys. At five they stopped for wine and pastries in a building that was older than Castle Vadim. Jon was called away to the phone. While the others lingered at the table, Carly wandered about, studying the architecture of the ancient building. She was startled to find herself being studied.

She turned around, and her eyes widened when she saw that the man behind her was a gray-haired hunchback. She tried to smile, while trying at the same time not to stare. He offered her a toothless grin and said, "You like?"

"The house?" Wishing her French were better, she tried to tell him it was very beautiful. *"Oui. Elle est très belle."*

He shrugged, and she saw that the man's eyes held a keen light of intelligence.

"Beautiful?" he said. "I don't know. But rich and fascinating—*mais oui!* Here, we are between the Dark Ages and the Renaissance. Our woods are misted, our forests deep. Mysteries surround our land. You'll note the pretty village—and that every pretty door carries a cross. Wherever you travel, you will find shrines— shrines to the Christ child, shrines to the Virgin Mary and shrines to all the saints of God!"

Little prickles of unease wound their way up Carly's spine. She had wandered into an archway now and could hear laughter in the distance. Tanya was teasing Alexi. They seemed so far away. Geoffrey said something to the two of them. Where was Jon?

"The count, he is a busy man," the hunchback warned her.

She nodded, shivering. She was being ridiculous, she chided herself. She stretched out her hand. "I'm Carly Kiernan. Is this your home and your business?"

He took her hand. His was gnarled but warm. "It is mine, yes. I am Henri Gasteau. Gasteaus have been here as long as Vadims have been here."

"That's wonderful."

"Where is your sister, Ms. Kiernan?"

"Jasmine?" she said, surprised.

"*Oui, madame.* She spoke often of your coming here. She was anxious to show you off."

"She—she left. She went on to Paris."

Gasteau blinked, and it was as if a curtain fell over his eyes. "She left . . . with you coming." He shrugged, smiling again. "Beyond is our enchanted forest, the land where the gray wolves roam and prowl and howl. Have you encountered any of our wolves, Madame Kiernan?"

"Yes, I have. They can be frightening."

"You must be very careful of creatures that suddenly appear in the woods, Madame Kiernan."

"I try to be careful. Always."

"Enjoy your stay, Madame Kiernan." He bowed to her and walked away.

She was still shaking, she realized. She hurried back to the table. Jon had returned. His eyes were sharp upon her as she sat down. She stared at the napoleon pastry she had ordered and could no longer eat. His knee brushed against hers, and she felt him still watching her. She couldn't look up, though she felt his gaze, the heat. Golden heat, like that in the hungry gaze of the wolf.

On the fourth day Jon decided that they would take a jaunt over the border. There was a slight cloud over it—he had to inform the inspector that they would be gone for a few days, but he promised he would return if he was needed for questioning.

Alexi, who invited himself along, was in an exuberant mood, and he dispelled all clouds of resentment and fear she felt as a result of the inspector's suspicions. They entered the Romanian province of Transylvania. Because she was with Count Vadim, Carly barely had to flash her passport at the border crossing.

The drive was long but intriguing. They headed for Brasov, one of Vlad Dracul's most famous haunts. They spent the first night in Siblu, a fairy-tale town that was said to have been Vlad Dracul's favorite. It was like a fourteenth-century cobbled kingdom, and Carly loved it. Jon was charming, and Alexi and Geoffrey both outdid themselves in telling her stories about the real count. He had supposedly been very handsome, pale, with curious green eyes. Eyes that could sometimes gleam gold, Alexi added.

Jon smiled at her apologetically. "They were hazel, really. Just ordinary hazel."

Tanya laughed and picked a flower, and Carly kept silent. There wasn't anything ordinary about him at all.

They spent two days in Sighisoara. Jon hired a young man, Michael—but he preferred "Micky"—to guide them. Micky convinced them that Sighisoara was one of the best-preserved fifteenth-century towns in Europe.

Geoffrey laughed and explained to Micky that Jon was the Count Vadim. Not wanting to insult the count's home Micky flushed and said that maybe they were both very well-preserved fifteenth-century towns. Jon agreed, and Micky proceeded to take them around.

"Vlad Tepes was born here," Micky informed them.

As they wandered along between buildings that seemed to meet over alleyways, Alexi told Geoffrey it would be a wonderful place to film a movie. Geoffrey reminded him that he directed plays.

"Yes, but there's always a first time for everything," Tanya commented, then shivered. "This place is delightfully gothic!"

"It gets better," Micky assured them. He led them onward, and they came to their destination—a yellowish house with a plaque that labeled it as the home where Vlad Dracul had been born in 1431. Upstairs there was a table set for lunch. While they were served a fiery plum brandy that Jon called *tuica*, gypsies began to dance. The dance was exciting, wild and fast and willful. Carly felt flushed and warmed by the brandy. She turned and found Jon watching her, smiling, his eyes heavy-lidded and sensual. He sipped his brandy, then reached out to her. She heard the plaintive cry of the violin and the crash of the tambourine just as he touched her lower lip and drew a finger across it. As she looked at him, she felt the fire of his eyes and the warmth of his nearness. She felt the promise of something that sizzled sweetly inside her. One day he would touch her further, she knew. She had never known anything as sweet or as painful as that anticipation.

He came closer to her; he parted her lips and kissed her lightly. Then he withdrew.

The violin rose to a high crescendo. A dancing girl called sharply and fell to the floor in a heap of colorful cotton. There was a burst of applause.

Carly drew her gaze away from Jon Vadim's and glanced up. An ancient picture of Vlad Dracul's father looked down grimly and mockingly upon her.

"Excuse me!" she murmured to no one in particular and left the table, searching out the ladies' room. She was grateful to find an ordinary rest room, where she splashed cold water on her face. Smiling, she felt that she'd made a return to the twentieth century and to sanity.

On the seventh morning the five headed out for another of Dracul's famous haunts—Brasov.

Along the way they passed cemeteries filled with fascinating old tombstones that were covered with beautiful flowers. The group passed a number of vineyards, rich and lovely against the backdrop of the mountains. The fall colors were still glorious, reds and golds and oranges abundant all around them.

Carly noticed signs on the road and asked about them.

Jon, driving, flashed her a smile. "They warn of Carpathian bears lurking in the woods."

"Here they warn of bears," Alexi murmured. "And at home we warn the unwary of the wolves that prowl about."

"In Manhattan we just warn people about the muggers," Carly said sweetly.

"In Manhattan the subways stand in for the forests," Geoffrey assured them all glumly.

Jon laughed. His hand found Carly's and he curled his fingers around hers.

They dined at a restaurant where bear steak was offered. Carly found the unusual entrée delicious, then wondered if it was the food or the company. Jon had set out to win her slowly, she realized, and it was a sweet and heady feeling. They were seated before a fire and served a wonderful warm ale. A stuffed bear loomed at the entrance, and hounds that were half wolf curled up by the fire. When they were done with the meal, Jon hired another tour guide, a middle-aged woman with silver hair. Her name was Dahlia, and as she took them through the town, she told them the story of Brasov, of how the people had refused to submit to Vlad Dracul. On August 24, 1460, Vlad Dracul therefore made Brasov famous for future generations by annihilating the population, impaling some thirty thousand men, women and children in a single day.

"How strange," Carly remarked. "It's such a lovely, lovely place today."

"With thirty thousand souls to haunt it!" Geoffrey teased her with a theatrical ghoulish laugh.

Tanya made a face at him and said, "What a despicable man! However did he earn such fame?"

"He was powerful. He fought the Turks and once killed twenty thousand Turkish soldiers in a field. It was two miles wide and half a mile deep. Mohammed II, the conqueror of Constantinople, who was quite a demon himself, was so stunned and repulsed by the sight of it that he retreated, rather than take on Vlad Dracul. He was cruel; he lived in a cruel age.''

''Do we ever get any better?'' Jon said softly.

Startled, Carly gazed at him. He smiled, shrugged and reached for her hand. The tour guide was watching them strangely, Carly noticed.

They returned to the restaurant. Just outside, the guide caught Carly's elbow. *''Noroc!''* she whispered tensely. *''Noroc!''*

''I'm sorry. I don't understand—'' Carly began, but Jon was paying the woman now, and she was smiling as she spoke with him rapidly in French.

''Alexi,'' Carly said, drawing the young man aside. ''Do you speak any Romanian?''

''A few words. Why?''

''What is *noroc*?''

He hesitated, watching her. ''Luck. It means luck. Why do you ask?''

''Oh, I just heard it,'' she said lamely. Chills swept along her spine, and she willed them to go away.

It had gotten quite late. Alexi suggested that they stay for the night, and they decided to do so. Tanya and Carly took a room together. In the middle of the night Carly awoke, hearing the cry of wolves.

She rose, went to the window and cast back the curtain to stare out into the night. She heard the fierce howling again. A cool breeze came in and swept around her. A light fog swirled below her on the ground.

''Carly!'' Tanya cried.

Carly was so startled that she uttered a little scream. Then both women laughed.

''Good heavens, what are you doing up?'' Tanya demanded.

''I heard wolves.''

"Well, really, this is Transylvania, remember? Close the window—you're supposed to be looking out for bats, not wolves. No, on second thought, I suppose a woman should always look out for wolves!"

They both smiled. Carly crept back into bed and finally drifted off.

She started to dream again. There was a wolf in her dream. A big, beautiful silver-gray timber wolf that ran fleet-footed and in silence through the mist. She could see his eyes and knew he was coming to her. The mist blurred, obscuring the wolf, and then he was no longer a wolf; he was a man.

Sleek, tall, naked, powerful and still fleet, he came for her. She knew that she should run, but she could not. She opened her arms, welcoming him.

She awoke, quivering. It was morning. Tanya still slept.

Carly rose and scrubbed her face with cold water, which helped a little.

It was very early, barely dawn. The one bathroom that served the three third-floor bedrooms would be empty. Carly was sure. She gathered her things and went inside to take a long, hot bath. She lay back in the water, trying to think. Something nagged at her, some feeling that things were still not right. Yet what could it be? She had met Geoffrey Taylor, and they liked each other very well, and she now had an important and exciting job for the spring.

She was in deadly danger of having an affair, she reminded herself. But she wouldn't think about that.

A man had been killed, she reminded herself.

But that just couldn't have anything to do with *them*. She so very badly wanted the magic to be real.

She toweled herself dry quickly—it was chilly in the bathroom. She dressed in a soft sweater and jeans, brushed her hair and applied a light makeup, then left the bathroom. She returned to their room, glancing at her watch, and sat down at the foot of the bed. Her dreaming had awakened her very early.

She wanted Jon Vadim, badly, she admitted. She shouldn't, but she did. And that was why she dreamed of wolves.

She should leave, go to Paris and look for her sister. Jasmine was still missing, and here she was, traveling around with Jon Vadim and company, without a care.

She would go to the inspector when they got back, she promised herself.

She wandered back to their third-story window and looked down. The woods were very thick, shadowed and a murky green, but there were also clear areas. She spied Jon just inside one of the clearings. His cheeks were clean-shaven, and his hair was damp, as if he, too, had just showered. He wore blue jeans and a navy sweater that brought out his coloring and breadth of his shoulders. He cupped his hands to light a cigarette, and then stared out at the day, exhaling slowly. He looked up then, as if he knew that Carly was there.

"Come down!" he quietly called to her.

She hesitated, reminding herself of Freud's theories about dreams. She should leave; she should run. He was a fascinating man, as beautiful, lithe and powerful as the running wolf, but he was still a wolf—and dangerous.

She smiled down at him, turned and left the room, with Tanya still sleeping. She ran down the quaint wooden staircase to the public rooms, then out the door and around the building and into the woods.

She spoke his name softly. She was surrounded by the trees, and the mist was still on the ground. As she moved along the trail that she was certain would lead her to him, the forest grew greener and darker.

"Jon!" she called.

Hearing a rustling sound, she remembered the signs on the road. She should beware of bears. And wolves. The dogs were bred with wolves here; wolf pelts lined the walls of the inn.

There was a sudden thrashing sound. "Jon!" she called out, panicking, and whirled.

He was running toward her, swift and beautiful and graceful.

"Carly, are you all right?"

She didn't say anything. She hurried to him and flung herself into his arms. He held her face, looked into her eyes and kissed her, and then put his arms around her again and captured her lips in a long, leisurely kiss. He held her tight while he tasted her. He brought her hips against his and gave her a hint of the hunger that he held in restraint. She slid against him at last, breathless, aware that her pulse was pounding, aware that her whole body ached with wanting. She knew she was playing games if she thought that she could deny this.

Holding her to him with his palm at the small of her back, he ran his knuckles over her cheek. "Little girls should always beware of the wolves in the forest, you know," he said lightly. "Unless they are willing to brave the wolf."

"Maybe," Carly murmured. She could feel the heat of him throbbing against her. She wanted to lie beside him in the mist on the forest floor. She wanted her dream to come to life, wanted to touch his naked flesh.

"Be very careful," he warned her, smoothing back a stray strand of her golden hair. "The wolf grows hungry."

"Does he?" Carly demanded, smiling lazily and arching against him.

He slipped his hand beneath her sweater and skimmed her flesh until he wrapped his fingers around her breast, teasing the flesh where it met the lace of her bra. He melded his lips with hers again. He found the snap of her bra and released it, then moved his palm over her nipple in a slow, sultry rotation that brought a whimper from her lips and a shaft of searing heat from her breast to the apex of her thighs. He pulled her even closer to him, and she felt the hardness of his arousal against his jeans. The heat of his kiss intensified. Entwined, she and Jon Vadim seemed to melt downward, to merge with the earth. On their knees, they fell into a soft pile of autumn leaves, gold and crimson, brilliant and beautiful. Continuing to kiss her, he laid her back and pushed up her sweater. She opened her eyes and saw the sky and the leaves and smelled the rich and redolent scent of the earth. He stroked her belly, and then she felt the liquid warmth of his kiss there. He unsnapped her jeans and massaged her flesh, stroking lower and lower with his hand as he moved his mouth over hers.

Hungrily.

He filled himself with her breasts, suckling one, then the other, first gentle in his touch, then slightly savage. Carly threaded her fingers through his hair, gasping, rocking on their bed of leaves. She wanted him, here, now, naked beside her. She had dreamed for so long. She didn't care that they were in the forest; it seemed the perfect place. The scent of the earth was as sweet and

natural as the longing that drew her to him, and it knew
nothing of time or place or manner or society or mores.
She had been waiting, and she could deny herself no
longer. The time was now.

He slipped her sweater over her shoulders, and her
bra fell free. As he pressed her back into the leaves, her
hair fell loose. Tense, unsmiling, he tangled his fingers
in the golden mass, spreading the tendrils further. Carly
watched him, but his gaze was on her bare breasts now.
He ran his forefinger over the shadowed valley between them. Lightly he placed his palms on her nipples, and she closed her eyes, quivering. When she
opened her eyes she saw the dappled sun beginning to
appear through the shadowed orange and gold of the
leaves and branches that formed the roof of their secret
bower. He cupped her breasts and teased the nipples
with his thumbs and forefingers. The sensation was excruciating as it rippled through her, causing a scalding
heat to sweep through her veins and pulse around her
heart and in the very core of her loins. She surged up to
meet him, but he pushed her back into the leaves. He
stared into her eyes, then pulled off his sweater and
came down on top of her. The feeling of his naked chest
brushing against her breasts was rough and so evocative that Carly was impelled to wind her arms around
his neck, trailing her fingers over his nape, kissing the
flesh of his shoulder. He held her and kissed her throat,
then buried his face against her shoulder, finding the
pulse in the hollow of her breasts. Carly cried out, not
knowing what she said, only that she begged him.
"Please..."

He pulled away from her. He rested on an elbow and
drew a finger from the valley of her breasts to the point

where the zipper of her jeans lay open. She shivered, feeling his relentless gaze and hard smile.

"Now, Carly, is the time to run. Maybe you have met a wolf in the forest. And maybe you should go. But now is the time to do it." He spoke harshly, but she didn't believe the ragged edge in his voice. He had to want her. She knew he felt the aching, too. He couldn't deny what she could reach out and touch if she dared.

He stared at her—hard. She shook her head, not knowing what to say. She felt exposed again as she lay there, half naked, on a bed of leaves. If he turned from her, she wouldn't be able to bear it.

She touched his face, resting her palm against his cheek. When he took her hand and kissed her palm, moving the tip of his tongue against it, she could scarcely breathe. She trembled on the brink. It had been so long, and she was so desperate, yet unsure of her ability to please.

It seemed as if he watched her forever. Dimly she became aware that the ragged sound of the wind was the sound of his breathing. His face was haggard with tension and desire.

Then suddenly he uttered an oath and fell upon her again, pinning her arms to the ground, taking her lips in a savage kiss. Down, down, into the bed of leaves they sank. His lips seared her mouth, face and throat, then he pulled away and stood. He kicked off his shoes and stripped away his socks and jeans and briefs. Carly lay still, mesmerized as she watched him with damp and swollen lips and an aching that burned the length of her body.

Naked, he was even more beautiful. He was the wolf, the wolf of her dreams become man, lithe and silent and sleek. He was completely tanned and muscled, and when he came down beside her again, she was trembling. Now he stripped away her sneakers and her socks, too, then peeled off her jeans, kissing her belly as he did so. Finally they were both naked in the forest, on the bed of crimson and golden leaves.

Kissing her, he stretched out alongside her. Then he caught her fingers in his and drew her arms high above her head. Balancing his weight upon one knee he moved with a supple rhythm as he kissed her lips and the pulse at her throat. She felt the hardness of him against her, and caught her breath. She felt the coldness of the air and the leaves beneath her, scratching at her flesh. She felt the heat of the sun and the blazing fire of his body as he rubbed against her. He freed her hands, then sat astride her, sweeping his own hands over her breasts, her midriff and her hips. Carly reached out and pulled him back to her. She gloried in the urgency of his kiss, and matched it. He caught her hair and smoothed it back, his features still tense.

"I have never been so...hungry," he told her. He searched out her eyes.

She could find her voice but not the words, and so she arched against him in response. He shifted smoothly and caught her knees, parted her thighs and wedged his body between them, still watching her. With a ragged sigh he ran his hands down her back and caught her buttocks, kneading them, lifting them.

He entered her very slowly, never losing eye contact with her. He sank into her as if fitting himself into a silken glove, slowly, slowly, filling her until she thought that she could take no more. But she was wrong, for her body accommodated him, and she was filled, as well, by the swift, fiery excitement and fever of it all. He withdrew and she was desolate; he advanced again, more fiercely, and she cried out. He withdrew once more, and then he filled her and filled her. At his urging she locked her limbs around his back, and the sweet teasing was over. He moved like a storm then, sweeping her away. The sensations overwhelmed her, freed her from herself. He took her with tenderness, but his hunger was savage and cast them rolling into the leaves. Colors tumbled around them, red, gold and crimson, and all in splendor. The colors wrapped themselves around her heart and warmed it just as the rhythm and fever of his thrust filled and warmed and caressed her body. She was aware of the scent of the leaves and the scent of the man, and then she was aware of nothing at all except for the release she strove so desperately to reach. When it burst upon her, it was liquid heat spilling from their loins. It was a spill of the colors of autumn, radiant and rich, red and gold and glowing.

But the day was cold. As Carly fell back to the bed of the earth, she became aware of the leaves beneath her, of the leaves tangled in her hair. She felt his hand on her abdomen, his dark head, damp against her chest. Idly he moved his fingers. He nuzzled her breast. She was alarmed at the rebirth of feeling that touched her instantly.

"We're in a bed of leaves, and you smell like roses," he murmured.

Carly stared up at the leaves overhead that blocked out the sun. "It was the soap," she replied.

He laughed, then rose above her, staring at her with blunt and keen appreciation. Having made love like a nymph in the leaves, Carly flushed. She rose on her elbows and looked for her sweater, but he pushed her back, falling beside her.

"Don't," he told her. "I want to hold on to this memory—your hair tangled in the leaves, your body so glorious against them, your eyes as turquoise as a tropical sea." He grinned. "You look great in leaves."

She flushed again. She wanted both to reach past him for her clothing and to run her fingers through the dark hair on his chest. Her second desire won out. She touched his chest, feeling the springy hair. "You don't look bad, in foliage, either, Count Vadim," she murmured, then hesitated before she said, "We should go back."

"Why?"

"Someone could—someone could come upon us here."

"In the woods?" he teased her. "Don't you know only wolves prowl the forest?"

"Hungry wolves," she said solemnly. Then she smiled, fascinated by the golden tenderness in his eyes. She had wanted him so badly and had finally had him, and the reality had exceeded every nuance of imagination. Or maybe she had never dared go quite so far in imagination. "Bears roam these woods, too," she said, remembering the signs.

"They wouldn't dare roam where this wolf has staked a claim," he told her with complete confidence.

She touched his face, her lips curled into a smile. "Are you a wolf?" she whispered.

"I am whatever you want me to be." His lips brushed hers, and he smiled. He was so striking, she reflected, with his damp dark hair falling over his forehead, his lip curled so ruefully. His body glistened with perspiration despite the coolness of the morning air. "I'm your lover now," he reminded her.

She wished she didn't color so easily. He found it amusing, she knew. "Yes," she said.

He chuckled softly. "I live in a castle and we're making love on the ground," he mused, then tensed. Moving over her again, he pushed back her hair, picking out the leaves, and kissed her lips, then her throat. "My God, you do smell like roses," he marveled. Carly felt him against her thighs, felt him hardening again. She made a little sound and wound her arms around him.

Their eyes met, and she felt somewhat dazed. She didn't believe their first passion could be relived, but her eagerness for this new encounter was as great as it had ever been. And the passion that tensed his features was every bit as strong.

Smiling at her, touching her, he whispered, "I warned you. You met a very hungry wolf in the woods, little girl."

"I'm not a little girl," she returned.

"No, you're not," he agreed, and his fingers danced over her curves, fondling her breasts. "No, you're not at all."

"I want—"

"What?" he demanded heatedly.

"I want . . . to touch you, too. I . . . I've dreamed of touching you."

"Then dream no more, my love," he told her with a husky note in his voice. He caught her hand and placed it against his chest, "Touch me and feel that this is real, that I am real."

Carly found greater courage—or greater imagination or maybe even a greater hunger—for she found it was easy to give free rein to her fascination, to explore him with abandon, with her fingers, with her lips. She bit at his shoulders, then bathed them with her tongue. She clung to him, arching upward. He murmured passionately at her touch. He finally pressed her back down, and she quivered and trembled, swept away once more, wondering if he did indeed mean to devour her, for his kiss consumed her. His touch was audacious now; his hands wandered everywhere. He stroked her thighs and thrust into her, and with a moan she curled against him, for he caught her tiny pebble of femininity and set her aflame again. She went to her knees, kissing him, catching his lower lip with her teeth, and raked her fingers down his back, no longer thinking of what she did when she grazed her nails over his hard-muscled buttocks.

And she didn't think, either, when she took him in her hands, stroking him. She grew bold, feeling as if the ancient magic of the forest invaded her soul, for she had never experienced a sensation so sweet, so all-absorbing, so commanding. He whispered to her, urging her on. His words grew rough and breathing came shallow and then he wrenched her into his arms and under him and seemed to burst within her. He fixed his mouth upon her breast as the storm of his ardor swept over them, and she cried out again and again as each wave crested, then exploded once again in the myriad colors of fall.

But this time when it was over he was silent. He drew her to him and stroked her hair, staring up at the sky. They lay that way until Carly shivered.

"You're cold," he said. He rose and found their clothing in the pile of leaves. He returned, smiling at Carly, and began to pick the leaves from her hair again. "I'm afraid I'll never really make you presentable," he said.

He dressed with confidence and economy of motion. Carly wasn't sure that she donned her clothing as gracefully. She longed for another bath. She tried to smooth back her hair and found more twigs. Jon pulled one off her sweater, smiling.

Tying her sneakers, she said uneasily, "I hope people are still sleeping. Everyone will..."

"Will what?"

She shrugged. "They'll know what we've been up to."

Laughing, he pulled her to her feet and drew her close. "I'm sure everyone has been wondering why it hasn't happened yet. My feelings for you are certainly obvious." He kissed her.

Carly gazed up at him, searching out his eyes. "Are you sure?..."

"Am I sure of what?" he demanded.

"Are you sure that you never... that you never had something—anything—going with Jasmine?"

"One more time, Carly. No. I did not."

He had to be telling the truth, she thought. He couldn't look at her so honestly and lie, could he?

He cupped her head with his hand and caressed her nape. "Have you enjoyed these days?"

She rested her palms against his chest. None so much as this one! she longed to admit. But she needed to keep her heart in reserve; she still didn't know where this passion and sweet obsession might lead. "Very much," she replied, and smiled. "Except that I'm scratchy as hell from all those leaves, and I'll never be able to get into the bath now."

"You picked the leaves, the time and the place. I would've been perfectly willing to share our first encounter on a bed. In fact, I tried for a first encounter on a bed.''

Carly lowered her lashes. "You don't understand—"

"I do understand," he told her gently. "And the time and the place were up to you. But you did pick the leaves."

"I suppose."

"Will you mind going home?" he asked.

"Home?"

"To the castle."

"No, of course not. Wait—yes! Perhaps I shouldn't go back to the castle. Not now—"

"Damn it, Carly, don't start that!" he said with annoyance.

Her eyes widened at the tone of his voice, and she started to push away from him, but he held her fast.

"You're too sensitive, and you have an outrageous temper," he said, laughing.

"I don't," she insisted.

"Then don't get mad over little things."

"But really—"

"I want to go back to the castle, Carly, so that you can take a bath whenever you like. Come on. Let's head back. We'll pack, and we can be home by tonight."

She found it difficult to resist his will. She had met her wolf in the forest at last, she realized, and the wolf had staked his claim.

And absurdly, she was thinking now, when it was way too late, that perhaps she should have run after all. He was a very demanding wolf.

Chapter 6

There was a small silver-gray car parked in the drive-
way when the five of them reached Castle Vadim late
that night.

Carly wasn't quite sure why, but as soon as she saw
the car, she felt an icy nail pierce her heart.

"The inspector's car," Jon murmured, frowning. He
seemed distracted. "I wonder what he's doing here."

He opened the car door for Carly. "Come on. Let's
see what has happened." He hurried along, practically
dragging her with him. Geoffrey, Alexi and Tanya followed.

They entered by the terrace, as usual. Marie was the
first to see them, and she welcomed Carly with a nervous *"Bonsoir"* and went on to speak rapidly to Jon in
an anxious tone. He nodded and again led Carly along
at an ungodly speed.

"What is it?" she demanded.

"Another murder," he said curtly.

Carly gasped, chills cascading down her spine. There had been so much magic.... But of course, she thought, magic was only pretense. It couldn't be real. They had left behind the enchantment when they'd reached the castle. Murder was real. And it cut between her and Jon Vadim as cleanly as a blade. She felt his withdrawal from her, felt the coldness and the hardness.

And she felt the fear within herself.

"Come on!" Jon urged her impatiently.

"Jon—" she started to protest. He still held her hand, but now the touch was cold. As cold as ice.

"Damn it, Carly, hurry. I want to know what happened this time."

"This time?"

He didn't say anything. They reached the library door, and Carly caught his hand before he could open it.

"Jon, talk to me! Why should the inspector be here? We've been gone a week. How could any of us be involved?"

"The girl has been dead over a week," he told her, then took her hand from his and opened the door.

Inspector LaRue was sitting on the corner of Jon's desk, pensively tapping his chin. When they came in he rose, extending a hand to Jon. "I'm sorry to greet you so, Count Vadim. I called this morning, and your maid said that you would return tonight."

Jon nodded. Carly thought he seemed wary. "You said we shouldn't go far—we didn't. Marie tells me that you've found a body."

LaRue nodded. "Just like the one last year."

"Last year?" Carly whispered.

The inspector stared at her. Carly wondered whether he read the relationship between them and pitied her for being fascinated by the count, a dangerous man. Suddenly she sensed that at best Jon would tire of her quickly and leave her.

At worst he might be a murderer.

"I'm sorry," the inspector said. "I did not mean to startle you, Madame Kiernan. I thought that your host might have mentioned the trouble last year."

Jon shrugged. "People die violently every day. I didn't know that I was obliged to tell Ms. Kiernan about them all."

"But Rochelle died here, Jon." The voice came from the doorway. It was Alexi, speaking apologetically.

"Rochelle?" Carly murmured.

"A very, very lovely little eighteen-year-old girl from the village who was working at the castle. She was found hideously mutilated in a cave in the woods. On the count's property," the inspector explained, watching Carly's reaction.

She hoped she appeared as impassive as Jon Vadim seemed to be. She was praying that no one would tell her that the count had been involved with the girl.

"And this time?" Jon asked.

The inspector reached into his suit pocket, found a picture and tossed it onto the desk. Everyone in the room—Jon and Carly, Alexi, and now Geoffrey and Tanya—moved forward. Tanya looked white and ill, and Carly realized that she herself probably looked ashen, as well.

The young girl in the picture had an abundance of blond curls and very dark eyes. She was laughing and looked very lovely.

"You found her where?" Jon asked.

"In the caves?" Alexi suggested uncomfortably.

"In the caves," the inspector said, picking up the picture as he shook his head unhappily. "So young, and so very beautiful." He pocketed the photo.

Jon walked across the room and reached into his bottom desk drawer for the brandy carafe and glasses. "Anyone?" he inquired politely.

Everyone nodded.

"You don't seem terribly concerned, Count," Inspector LaRue said reproachfully.

Carly lowered her head as she accepted a glass of brandy from Jon. She had to agree with the inspector. Jon took his time before answering. He was watching her reaction carefully, but didn't seem shocked or horrified. Rather, she thought, he seemed cold. He left Carly and offered glasses of brandy to the others.

"Au contraire, mon ami," Jon replied at last. He tilted his head and drank his brandy, then set the glass back on his desk with a sharp crack. "I am very concerned. It is my property, of course. And it is I whom you seem to be accusing."

"I am not making accusations."

"Then you are making insinuations, and I resent them heartily."

"I am asking questions. I must. The coroner thinks the girl was killed a week to ten days ago. She was viciously mauled, her throat torn as if an animal had ripped it apart."

"You're sure that it wasn't wolves?" Geoffrey inquired.

"Wolves do not strip their victims and lay them out with the arms folded and the fingers entwined as if in prayer, Monsieur Taylor. No, it is the work of a man," the inspector replied.

"Or a woman," Tanya suggested.

The inspector stared at her sharply. "What made you say that?" he snapped.

Tanya almost jumped. "I don't know! Because it's a liberated world, I suppose."

Inspector LaRue turned his sharp gaze upon Carly. "You have not heard from your sister, Madame Kiernan?"

"Er, no. No, I haven't," Carly admitted. She looked guiltily from the inspector to Jon. He was staring at her. Coldly. Now he had erected a wall against her just as he had done with the inspector. He smiled, cruelly, mockingly, and looked back at the inspector.

"I think that Ms. Kiernan will find a note from Jasmine in her room."

"What?" Carly cried out.

"Marie told me that a forwarded letter has reached you at last. It went to your home, then to the American Express office in Vienna, and now it has come here."

Carly swung around, looking at the inspector. "May I?"

He lifted his hand. "Of course. I would like any light possible shed on this situation."

Carly nodded and ran out of the room.

The upstairs was dimly lit. Walking along the beautiful corridor, with its ancient marble flooring, she started to shiver as the reality of it all hit her. A year ago someone had cruelly murdered a young girl, stolen life and beauty and innocence. And now it had happened again. Here.

And the inspector obviously suspected Jon Vadim.

Carly paused at her door. Her heart was beating furiously. Was she a fool? Was she so immersed in falling in love with the man, in falling beneath his spell, that she couldn't see the truth? Was he a heinous murderer?

He had warned her that he was a wolf, a wolf prowling the forest. And wolves could be dangerous. She remembered that the two girls had had their throats ripped out as if an animal had attacked them....

"No!" she whispered, opening the door to her room. She paused when she heard a soft whirring sound. Again, an awful feeling of cold panic possessed her as if icy fingers were closing around her heart, around her throat. Someone was in her room. Someone silent, someone furtive.

Forcing herself to move, she turned on the overhead light. The room was flooded with sudden brilliance.

It was empty. The French doors from the terrace were closed and locked. Her suitcase from the trip lay on the rug at the foot of her bed.

Gathering her courage, she hurried across the room to the bathroom, clicking on the light. The bathroom, too, was empty.

She sighed and nearly sank to the floor on wobbly knees. She pressed her hands against her cheeks and found them cold. She was imagining things, she told herself. She had imagined the whirring sound, and she had imagined that someone had been here.

She forced herself to turn around. She hurried to the dresser, where she found the letter that Jon had referred to. She cried out when she saw it—the handwriting was definitely Jasmine's, and it bore at least half a dozen different postmarks. The village had forwarded it here. She picked up the letter and anxiously slit it open.

Carly,
I've been trying to call you all night. Where have you been? You know how I hate to write, but this

is important. Don't come! Please don't come here.
I know that this sounds crazy, but I'm leaving myself. There might be some danger. Sounds terribly
gothic and dramatic, doesn't it? But you know me.
Love you, sis. Stay home, and I'll make it all up to
you. I promise.
Jasmine

She reread it, then turned it over in her hands to study
the postmarks. She had to admit it seemed as if Jon was
telling the truth.

A slight noise startled her, and she almost screamed.
She brought her hand to her throat as she stared at the
doorway.

The hall was still shadowed, so that the man standing there was nothing more than a silhouette that
seemed to fill the doorway with his presence. She realized quickly that it was Jon. He was the man she had
wanted so badly that she had gladly lain down with him
on the bare earth in a bed of fall leaves, and suddenly,
despite Jasmine's letter, she was frightened of him.

"Did you find it?" he asked, moving toward her.

Carly nodded, unable to speak.

"May I?" He reached for the letter. Smiling, he
moved his hand to the nape of her neck in an idle caress. She didn't mean to jerk away, but she did.

His gaze left the letter and fell on her. His lip curled,
and he dropped his hand, then returned his attention to
the letter. "Thank God," he murmured. "At least this
puts me in the clear on the matter of Jasmine."

"Yes," Carly said. As he stared at her, she couldn't
smile, and she couldn't pretend that she wasn't numb.

His lip remained locked in the derisive curve as he
asked, "May I give this to the inspector?"

"Yes, yes, of course."

He moved aside, indicating with a sweeping gesture that she should precede him. She did so. She wanted to turn around and say that she was sorry, except she wasn't quite sure what she was sorry for. She was painfully confused. She couldn't believe he could be a murderer. But she was afraid, anyway, mainly because she had been falling in love, so deeply and so completely that she just might believe in his innocence because she was blinded by that love.

She knew he was walking close behind her. She felt the warmth of his breath against her skin. On the stairway, he drew level, though he didn't touch her. They didn't speak until they had returned to the library.

Tanya was on either her second or third brandy. Alexi and Geoffrey both looked up guiltily, as if they had been discussing Jon.

"So," the inspector said. "This letter has not disappeared."

"No. It's very much here," Jon said.

Inspector LaRue read the letter quickly. He looked at Carly. "It seems that she is well enough—somewhere."

"Yes, I most certainly hope so," Carly said.

"She mentions danger," LaRue said to Jon.

Jon sighed with exasperation. "Jasmine is one of the most dramatic people I have ever met. She thrives on any kind of excitement. I have no idea what she is referring to."

"Why did she leave so hastily when she was planning to be here for your party?" the inspector inquired.

"I don't know."

"I understand you had a falling-out."

Jon cast a sharp gaze toward Alexi, then narrowed his eyes on Geoffrey. "I don't know what was said. Jasmine and I had no argument. Her sister will tell you. Jasmine does have a quick temper. If she wasn't pleased with some arrangement I made, she might easily have decided to leave."

Inspector LaRue nodded and smiled. "I understand that she ran screaming from the stables just days before the party."

Jon was still for a minute, his features tense. He shrugged. "Something startled her."

"Perhaps someone attacked her," the inspector suggested.

Jon threw up his arms. "Are you ready to arrest me, Inspector? If not, I'm tired, and I'm weary of innuendo and insinuation. Please, if there is nothing more concrete.... It is late."

"No, no, there is nothing." The inspector bowed slightly to the group. "I will, however, appreciate it if you all stay close at hand. Please, don't cross any borders." Shaking his head, he smiled at Carly. "What puzzles me is that I can't seem to find any record of your sister having crossed the border into any other country."

"What?" Carly said worriedly.

"That's no great dilemma," Jon said flatly. "They barely glance at the passports half the time when we drive from country to country."

"But Jasmine carries an American passport, and in this region they are stricter with Americans."

"Jasmine could bat her lashes and go anywhere she wished," Jon said dryly.

Carly felt cold waves envelop her again. He sounded as if he knew her sister so well. But he had denied that they'd had a relationship. And she had believed him.

She suddenly sank into one of the plush library chairs. She wanted to talk to her sister, wanted to have her right in front of her, in the flesh. She was frightened, and only Jasmine's appearance could change that. Two women and a man were dead, and she had almost been killed in a coach herself. Though she hadn't wanted to admit it before, she knew Tanya had implied that there had been something between Jon and Jasmine.

"Good night," the inspector was saying.

Carly looked up. He was leaving. Jon accompanied him. When the door closed behind them, Geoffrey, Alexi, Tanya and Carly stared at one another in a complete and explosive silence.

"Oh, don't be absurd!" Tanya burst out. "Jon did not do it!"

Carly felt she herself should have been the one saying it.

"Of course he didn't," Geoffrey agreed. He stood up, stretching, and walked across the room to pour himself another brandy. He leaned against the desk and smiled around the room at them. "Heck, if being here is the only motive, every single one of us was here last year, too, when the other girl was murdered. Except for Carly, of course. But then, Jasmine was here last year. Carly is taking her place." He smiled at her, lifting his glass to her. "To Carly, the one and only innocent among us."

"The lamb to the wolves!" Tanya agreed.

"Hear! Hear!" Alexi said.

Carly jumped to her feet. "Stop it, will you! This is tragic!"

Geoffrey sobered quickly. "I'm sorry, Carly. You're still worried about Jasmine, aren't you?" He came over and squeezed her hand. "Jasmine is fine. I promise you." He yawned. "I'm going up. Excuse me, will you all?"

Tanya, too, stood, staring at Carly and Alexi almost belligerently. "I'm going up, too. I'm exhausted. Please, say good-night to Jon for me."

She followed Geoffrey out of the room. Carly hadn't been able to move.

Alexi poured fresh brandies for himself and Carly, then forced the glass into her numb fingers. "It's all right. Really, it's all right."

She gazed up at the handsome, earnest young man. "Why is the inspector so down on Jon?"

Grimacing, Alexi hesitated as if trying to elude the question. "Well, the family is old, you know. Older than the legends of Vlad Dracul. They've been counts of this region before Christianity was even embraced here."

Carly shook her head. She swallowed the brandy and felt somewhat warmed. "That doesn't mean anything. Innumerable families in Europe go back for centuries. The inspector wouldn't be suspicious of Jon because of that."

Alexi sighed. "Well, Carly...."

"Alexi, damn it, why are you hedging?"

He waved a hand in the air. "Legend, you know."

"No, I don't know."

"This is a place of fog and mist and ancient superstition. The wolves howl at the full moon. The people keep crosses on their doorways, and they say their Hail Marys before they travel through the woods."

"Go on," she prompted him.

"There are legends of man-beasts. Of creatures part wolf and part human—"

"Oh, Alexi!" Carly protested. "You're calling Jon a werewolf? Oh, please!"

Alexi flushed. "No, I'm not calling Jon a werewolf. I'm just saying that this is a legend-filled place. People believe in magic, and in good and evil. They believe in spells, in curses." He hesitated. "There is a disease, you know."

"A disease?" Carly asked warily.

"Lycanthropy. It is documented. People have thought that they were part wolf. There was one very famous case here. In the 1850s. A poor, demented fellow thought that he was a wolf. He tore apart twenty young men and women before he was caught in the act of eating a human heart. He only killed by the light of the full moon. They knew he was horribly insane, but in those days he was sent to the gallows."

A harsh sound of impatience from someone else in the room startled Carly so that she cried out, spilling her brandy as she leaped from her chair.

Jon had come upon them, having returned in silence, and now stared at the two of them with naked fury.

"Alexi, what the bloody hell are you telling her?" Jon's voice sounded like a growl.

"Nothing." Alexi shook his head and cast Carly a quick, apologetic glance. "Just a little local legend, that's all. Jon, really, think about it. These murders just aren't normal!"

Jon walked around the desk and sank into his chair. His gaze fell on Carly, and she couldn't pull her own away. Her heart was beating rampantly, and she didn't know whether it was from fear or desire. His eyes mocked her, challenged her. She stared at the sensual fullness of his lips and remembered their touch. She could almost feel the caress of his hands. She remembered his smile, his laughter, the tension and the sweet, heady passion, and she felt as if lava flowed inside of her again.

She wanted to see Jasmine, she reminded herself. She tore her gaze away, because she gave too much too quickly. She was, perhaps, too innocent for this game.

A lamb to the wolves, she thought.

She jumped to her feet. "I'm going to bed."

Jon picked up a pencil and idly scratched on the blotter before him. "Carly, stay, please," he said. It was another command. He grinned lazily at Alexi. "Alexi, if you wouldn't mind? I assume you're staying; it is late. But if you'll excuse us, I'd like a minute alone with Carly."

"Of course. Of course," Alexi said. He looked unhappily at Carly. Carly wished she'd bolted when she'd had the chance.

"I'm really tired, too, Jon—" she began to say, but he was already on his feet. Swiftly he moved around the desk and put himself between Carly and the door. She felt that if she tried to leave he would stop her physically, not giving a damn that Alexi was with them.

"I will leave you," Alexi said. He looked from one of them to the other as he backed out of the room. Jon said good-night to him but never lifted his gaze from Carly's. Her heart leaped into her throat. She couldn't move. She watched the ripple of muscle beneath his denim shirt and remembered how he'd looked, how he'd felt, and how very intimate they had been. She wanted to run to him and bury her face against him. She wanted him to touch her again.

He lifted her chin, and she feared he hadn't forgiven her. He very lightly kissed her lips, and pulled her near.

"You're afraid of me," he said flatly.

"No."

"You're a liar."

"I'm not lying. I just . . ."

"You just what?"

"Nothing." She didn't know what to think or feel. His arms were around her, his body was pressed against hers, and there was a new intimacy to the hold, for they both knew how very well they fitted together. The brandy was blurring her senses, but she thought that she would always know the subtle, masculine scent of him and the tension and electricity that abounded in him. If she left him now, she would always remember the hypnotic quality of his eyes and the power of his voice. Logic fled. She wanted to believe. She did believe. And she was trembling.

He drew his thumb slowly over her lower lip, watching the movement with fascination. She gazed into his eyes, and they grew darker, like molten honey, and his smile deepened wickedly.

"You are afraid, and you should run," he said. "Fly—all the way home. Back to your safe little harbor in New York."

"You want me to leave."

He shook his head. "I want you . . . here. Beside me. Beneath me. But maybe you should listen to the things you hear. Maybe you are a lamb cast into a den of wolves."

"Perhaps I'm not so fragile."

"You are frightened," he stated.

"I have a right to be frightened."

His smile belied his tension. He trembled slightly, and she didn't know whether it was from passion or anger. He moved his thumbs over her cheeks, and she stared at him, mesmerized. From head to toe, she realized, he was taut. Like an animal on the prowl.

"Then go," he told her. "I don't want any woman who feels she must shrink from me when I touch her." He released her. She heard sharp disappointment in his voice as he said, "Go. Go, Carly. Go up to bed and lock your door."

"From you?" she demanded hoarsely. She was angry and hurt, and she hated her confusion and the pain. He didn't reply, and she swept past him. "I'll be out of here in the morning."

"To leave for the States?"

"No. I want to see my sister."

"Then you won't be leaving. I promise you."

When she reached the door, she turned and offered him a cool, polite smile. "My door will be locked."

He answered with a tilt of his head. "Don't be foolish. If I wanted you now, I would have you now. I'm the one person you can't lock out. But go. Run. Be a good little lamb and run as fast as you can."

Carly uttered an expletive and rushed out of the room, slamming the door behind her. The hallway was empty, and very lonely. She was tempted to turn around, to apologize. Something warned her that she couldn't. There were too many unanswered questions.

She ran through the terrace. It was eerie by night, half lit, for the full moon had waned to three quarters. Mist was rolling in, touching everything.

Carly raced up the stairs. Fear skipped along her spine as she heard the first howl of the wolves. When she reached her room, she slammed the door and locked it.

Her heart beating rapidly, she quickly checked out the bathroom, then sighed and sat down at the foot of the bed. She crossed her arms over her chest and huddled there, trying to think.

This was so very different. It was like a flash fire, an explosion of desire and emotion, and it frightened her. She had been in love before, deeply in love. But that love had come slowly and had not been touched by shadows.

Even death had come slowly then. She had fought cancer with Tim for a long time. She had lived endlessly with the effort and the fight and the pain, and then she had lived with the grief. She had been cocooned for the longest time, protected from caring.

And now this . . .

She'd never imagined a desire so strong. She had never thought that she would be able to lie with a man and lose herself within him so completely. There had been no shyness, no awkwardness. From the first moment she had seen him, she had wanted him, for in that first moment she had begun to fall in love with him.

Her heart sank with horror. Two girls had been killed, and Jasmine was missing. Carly was afraid to give form to her thought.

She might very well be in love with a maniacal killer who had caused her sister's disappearance.

"No!" She formed the word in silence and started to shiver. He wanted her to go away. No, he wanted her to stay. He wanted her. None of it had changed. She had changed, and he had known and had pushed her away in anger.

Carly got up to check the bolt on her door. She checked the French doors, and they, too, were locked. She changed into her flannel nightgown and crawled into bed. She wouldn't sleep, she thought. She was too frightened.

She did sleep, though, and her dream came back to her, her dream of the wolf. The beautiful silver-gray wolf who ran toward her and slipped through the mist and became a man. Jon. Tonight the dream didn't stop. He took her into his arms and carried her off into the clouds. And he made love to her with a sweet, rough magic, for he was savage and tender all at once, gentle and yet hungry, as the wolf was hungry....

She twisted, fighting the dream as she slept. She forced herself to awaken.

His scent was on the air.

She was still dreaming, she told herself. It must be the brandy.

She opened her eyes wide in the darkness, trying to tell herself that she was imagining the subtle, pleasant, evocative and masculine scent that she had come to know so very well. But mist or magic, it was there.

She said his name aloud and sat up and switched on the light. The room was empty.

Carly bolted out of bed and checked the door and then the bathroom. No one was there, yet, unless she had completely lost her mind, some presence of his lingered.

A gust of wind suddenly opened the terrace doors. Carly screamed and then saw that the terrace was empty. The sky was pink and gray, and the cold wind was sweeping by her again. A storm was brewing.

She hurried over to the doors and pushed them shut, straining against the force of the wind. She paused, and the doors flew open again and the wind swept by her. She stood on the terrace and looked down.

The wolf was there. *A* wolf, she told herself numbly. A big silver-gray wolf sat far below her in the courtyard. It cast back its head and howled. The sound was eerie and plaintive. The animal looked up. Carly could have sworn that it stared straight at her. It howled again, then it turned and ran. Sleek and beautiful and powerful, it headed into the woods.

The wind picked up again, cold with the promise of winter. It tugged at Carly's hair, stung her eyes and sent her gown rippling about her legs.

She came back inside, forcing the doors closed. She set the bolt, but she knew that another gust of wind could open the doors again, so she dragged the dresser chair over and set it before the windows.

Shivering, she crawled back into bed and pulled the covers around her. She finally realized that she was frightened, very frightened. She had to leave. She was going mad here. She was really beginning to wonder if the man she loved was really a beast. A silver-gray wolf with haunting golden eyes.

Chapter 7

Carly did not leave in the morning.

She slept late. When she awoke, she was still drowsy and tired, and therefore irritated that she'd dreamed of a silver wolf and imagined that a man had come to her by night, silent, watching her, then slipped away, leaving behind just a hint of his presence....

The world seemed entirely silent, then she heard a sound down in the courtyard. She went to the window. Jon was down there, mounting Satan. Even as she watched he rode off, disappearing into the woods as the wolf had done.

She stayed there for some time, looking after him. She really should go. The inspector didn't want her to leave the duchy, but she could check into the hotel in the village again. Maybe once she was away she wouldn't dream of magnificent beasts with golden eyes. Maybe she wouldn't imagine that a man was with her. Maybe she could shake the hypnotic spell of Jon Vadim.

A man suspected of horrible murders.

She shook her head to herself, denying it. She was in love with him; she could admit it freely to herself. If she loved him, she owed him some kind of faith.

She wasn't leaving. Not then. Maybe later.

Carly dressed and wandered down to the terrace. The only one there was Geoffrey. He was sipping a cup of coffee and reading a manuscript. He looked up when she came, smiling.

"Carly. Welcome. It was kind of lonely here."

"You look busy."

"I'm not. Sit down, please."

Carly sat down. A maid seemed to materialize from the corners of the room to ask Carly what she would like for *le petit déjeuner*. Carly asked for some coffee and toast, and once it came and she and Geoffrey were alone together, she asked him what he was up to.

"It's the script for my next play," he told her, smiling. "Our next play. You are going to work for me?"

Carly nodded with pleasure. She was still a little in awe of the fact that he had liked her costume for the party enough to hire her for his next period piece with no more effort whatsoever. He grinned, pleased with her response. "I'll give you the play to read." He shrugged. "Might as well use some of our time wisely."

Carly sipped her coffee.

"How long were you planning on staying here?" she asked him.

"Well, I don't have to be back until January 15— which is when I'll need you, by the way. Fittings and all. You'll see how extensive the wardrobe is once you've read through the play. It's a good thing time isn't of the essence. I think that inspector would find a way to arrest us all just to keep us here, though God knows why."

Carly didn't know why, but she felt it necessary to defend Inspector LaRue. "People have died. He has to find out what's happening."

Geoffrey smiled at her, sitting back. "Carly to the rescue! Jasmine said that you could be fierce in the crusade for others."

"I'm not crusading. I'm..."

"Frightened?"

"No, not really," she protested, a shade too quickly.

He shrugged. "Well, don't let them scare you. I've known Jon a long time. He's no maniacal murderer—no matter what Alexi says."

"What does Alexi say?"

"Oh, you know. All that rot about lycanthropy and werewolves and all. These people are too superstitious."

"They're charming people."

"There you go again, the sweet crusader."

"I'm so terribly sweet," Carly assured him. She nibbled thoughtfully at her toast and felt him watching her with an amused smile. "I'm not, really."

"Okay, you're the Witch of the West. Whatever you want."

She laughed, feeling better. Geoffrey had defended Jon and had been down-to-earth, and she just felt more—normal. "I just wish Jasmine would call," she murmured, as much to herself as to him.

She expected an assurance from him. It didn't come. She looked at him at last, and he seemed somewhat pensive himself. "Geoffrey?" she asked.

"I don't know. Jasmine is like the wind. She's beautiful, and we all love her. But she does move like wildfire. Still..."

"Still, what? Geoffrey, please?"

"Well, I just thought . . . there had been a time there when she and Jon . . ."

"When she and Jon what?" Carly demanded.

"Oh, nothing," he said, but she thought he looked slightly guilty. "She and Jon planned the party together. Jon never minds that she brings in so many people, because they all donate to charities to attend. But it is Jasmine's bash. And this year, of course, she had invited you."

"Yes, of course," Carly said. "Geoffrey, is that all?"

"Is that all? Of course that's all," he assured her.

She wished she believed him. She couldn't help but wonder again about her sister and Jon Vadim. Everything hinted that the two of them had enjoyed a very close relationship. But Jon had denied it.

Please, let him be telling the truth! Carly prayed in silence. Geoffrey was staring at her. She hoped that he wasn't pitying her for falling so very hard.

"Well, Jon is off riding and Tanya and Alexi still seem to be sleeping," he said brightly. "I think I'll take a jaunt into the village. Want to come?"

Carly didn't think she had the energy. She hesitated, then thanked him for the invitation and told him no, that she would like to read the play. He offered her the script and left her at the terrace table. She stared blankly at the page, realizing that she was anxious to see Jon.

When she did see him that night, he was aloof and distant, and in return she was defensively cool and equally distant. She managed to excuse herself early and escaped to her room. She realized as she lay on the bed and stared at the ceiling that she wanted him to come to her. She wanted him to lay his heart at her feet and swear again that he was innocent. She wanted to believe him. She wanted to pretend that none of it had happened, that the magic had all been real, that she was really like the Cinderella who had entered an enchanted carriage and been swept off her feet by a prince.

It wasn't his title that she liked, or the coach or the castle or anything else tangible. It was the love she craved, the intimacy that had been so briefly hers—only to be snatched away.

But she remembered with a sharp twist of pain that she didn't trust him—that she would be horrified if she had merely provided entertainment to fill the void left by her sister.

And then again—where *was* Jasmine?

Again she fell asleep telling herself that she should leave. Again when she woke, she did nothing toward leaving the castle. She dressed in jeans and went down to the terrace for breakfast, hoping to see Jon. But he wasn't there; he was closeted in the library with the inspector, or so Tanya told her. Tanya was bored. When they had nibbled at fresh croissants, she decided to take Carly on a tour of the castle.

Carly loved it. They explored the grand ballroom, music gallery, the solarium, and the newer rooms: the men's gallery, put in during the last century, and the ladies' bower, added in the 1930s. Upstairs, Tanya giggled when Carly refused to enter Jon's room. It was a wonderful bedroom, right out of a fantasy—or the *Architectural Digest*. Rows of French doors opened onto a long terrace, and there was a round dais for the massive old bed, with its dark wooden canopy and intricately carved posts. There was also a long, heavy oak desk, comfortable chairs stood before the fireplace, and there was a small, circular table with a pair of chairs for intimate dining.

"Want to go through his drawers?" Tanya asked.

"No!" Carly insisted, and Tanya grinned wickedly. Carly would really have loved to have gone through his things. But it was painful to be there, too. She had seemed so close to him but hadn't gotten close at all. She wanted to reach out and touch him again, but she couldn't allow herself to do so. She couldn't be a fool; she knew her wariness of him was well warranted, and he had to realize that he owed her a number of explanations.

He wasn't giving her any explanations.

At dinner that night, he was the perfect host. Carly decided not to escape to her bedroom; she wanted to be near him.

But that night Jon escaped. He left them all at the table, and while conversation flowed easily enough around her, Carly felt acutely uncomfortable. While coffee and dessert and brandy and liqueurs were served, she felt pricks of unease against her spine, as if they were being watched.

That night she dreamed of the wolf again, coming toward her, running through the mist. He came nearer and nearer, and his coat was lush and silver.

And his eyes were gold.

She wanted him so badly that she lay still. She saw the cunning in his golden eyes and sensed the danger. But she waited. And when he drew near, she stretched out her arms. He leaped through the mist, powerful, lithe. And then he was a man, still taut and sinewed and majestic, with masculine grace and power. She reached for him. She nearly cried out when he came to her, and she didn't care if he was man or beast, only that he touched her again, that he loved her again.

Days passed in miserable tension. Carly read the play and explored the basement with Tanya and Alexi. Carly could see that no Vadim had much cared about the basement in decades. There was a crypt there that hadn't been used in several centuries. A wall sealed off the ancient dead, much to Carly's comfort.

But beyond the wine cellar, in musty rooms where spiderwebs covered the corners and crevices, were the old dungeons, and deep in the bowels of the castle lay a room where "unfortunates" had once been housed. They had been pathetic creatures drawn into the Inquisition, petty criminals who had dared defy their counts. Carly saw the remains of a rack, covered with centuries of dust, an iron maiden, an assortment of whips and chains and scolds' bridles, thumbscrews and mammoth pinchers.

"Nice people, eh?" Alexi whispered with a wicked laugh.

Carly didn't even try to smile. She didn't like the basement. "Someone should really clean this place out."

"Oh, don't be silly," Tanya protested. "These pieces are of great historical value."

"Then they should be in a museum," Carly said.

Alexi was amused. "Do I detect a note of fear? Think of it—the long-lost relations of our dear count used to come down here to inflict torture. Behold, my dears, the iron maiden. That charming piece of steel could crush a man, and this particular model could disembowel him—or her—in the process."

The room was dim. Electric lights had been strung out, but their glow was pale. There were bloodstains in the stone, sins the Vadims might well have wanted hidden.

Carly shivered. She wanted to go back upstairs.

A voice cut into the darkness. "Sightseeing?"

She yelled, jumping. Tanya, too, was startled enough to cry out.

It was Jon. He had come upon them silently and was standing before one of the naked light bulbs, so that Carly could not see his face. He sounded angry again, but his anger was dry and cold and ironic. For a moment they all drew back, awed by the suddenness of his appearance and the larger-than-life figure he created.

As he walked in to join them he blew the dust off a wickedly knotted whip and picked it up. "I imagine this one could strip flesh from bone," he said. He cracked the weapon in the air, and the sudden noise drew a gasp of protest from Carly. His eyes found hers, but there was no warmth in them. They assessed her swiftly. He set the whip down. He smiled at Alexi. "You're being very dramatic again, my friend. You know that none of the counts or even the family actually practiced torture."

His expression unreadable, he turned to Carly and Tanya. He smiled, and his teeth flashed white against the striking bronze of his features. "We merely picked out the victims—then we ordered our henchmen to strip their flesh from their bones."

They stared at him silently. It had to be the mood of the place, Carly decided.

"Do enjoy yourselves," he said, and left, his shoes striking the stone sharply.

Tanya shivered. "Boy. I think he was mad."

"How did he come, without our hearing him?" Alexi murmured.

Jon's footsteps still echoed against the stone. Carly thought of a wolf padding silently through the forest. Then she flushed, embarrassed. They were prowling around his home, condemning his ancestors. "Let's get out of here," she urged.

"Mais, oui. Allons-y," Alexi agreed.

Geoffrey was alone when Carly reached the terrace for dinner that evening. She told him what had happened, wondering if they had offended Jon.

Geoffrey shrugged. "I doubt it. Alexi is always dramatic."

"Yes, but have there always been corpses around?" Carly asked uncomfortably.

Geoffrey didn't answer for a moment. "No," he said at last, then sighed. "I wish that the inspector would find out the truth, instead of harassing Jon. Then we could all go home and Jon would be left in peace."

"What's that?" Jon said, arriving on the terrace. "Do I need peace?"

They turned around. That afternoon he had been dressed casually, in jeans and a sweatshirt. Now he was all male elegance, in a black tuxedo, silk shirt and tie and velvet vest. He came toward them, smiling vaguely, swirling amber Scotch in a rock glass.

"Carly was concerned for you," Geoffrey said.

"Was she?" Jon inquired, smiling pleasantly, his gaze focused on her. "How nice."

She returned his stare steadily but said nothing. He shrugged and turned back to Geoffrey to say, "You missed the excursion into the realm of darkness."

"I've been on Alexi's tours to your basement before," Geoffrey reminded him.

"Ah, yes. That's right."

"If it bothers you, you should get rid of it all!" Carly charged him.

"Yes, ma'am, Ms. Kiernan!"

"I really don't see that it is a joking matter." She stood her ground, challenging him. But then she thought about the basement, about the meandering corridors and the stale, musty scent, the walls that sealed off entire sections of—bodies.

There could be newer bodies there, she thought. In the endless shadowy archways, murder could take place. A victim could lie for days, for months, without being found.

She realized he must have read her mind, for his lids flickered briefly and he walked by her, pulling back a chair for her to sit at the table. He gazed at her with the cool disdain that meant he knew her fears and did not forgive her for them.

Carly didn't move at first. His smile deepened, and she brushed by him as she took her seat. She felt his breath at her nape as he pushed in the chair, and a trembling took hold of her. In seconds her imagination was running wild. Alexi and Tanya were walking in, but she almost cried out, anyway. She almost leaped to her feet, almost touched his shoulders, almost shook him.

Just talk to me! she wanted to scream. Tell me the truth. Tell me what's going on! Because there was, beyond a doubt, something here that he understood while she did not.

She envied Tanya, who was easily kissing Jon's cheek. "You old grouch! I'm terribly sorry about this afternoon. I really didn't have the right to go wandering, but honestly, love, you were a total bear."

"Tanya, this is my home."

Tanya sat down and began buttering a roll. "Yes, but really, Jon, those are museum pieces. You could preserve them and send them to some deserving institute."

She lifted her wineglass to Carly. "The Smithsonian! The Americans love things like that!"

"And the British don't?" Geoffrey asked her.

She laughed. "Oh, we thrive on such stuff. But then, we have tons and tons of our own."

Alexi laughed and Jon offered an honest smile and the evening progressed nicely. Carly wondered if there wasn't some way to talk to Jon. But when the meal was over, Jon was summoned to answer a phone call. Alexi and Geoffrey started a game of chess, and Tanya grew bored. Carly tried to keep talking to her. For an hour Tanya responded, but then she yawned and said that she was going upstairs. Alexi checkmated Geoffrey at last, and the men decided to go to bed, too. Carly said that she was going to sit on the terrace awhile longer.

Jon didn't return.

At last she went to the library. She heard voices, and one was definitely Jon's. She couldn't follow the conversation, though, for the rapid, impassioned words were French.

She started to knock on the door, then hesitated. She raised her hand again and knocked. Suddenly determined to know whom Jon was arguing with, she pushed open the door.

Jon was sitting behind his desk. He was in a terry robe and wearing dark-rimmed reading glasses.

And he was alone.

"Madame Kiernan," he murmured. "Is something wrong?"

Carly looked around the room. "Please, don't 'Madame Kiernan' me, Jon. Who were you arguing with?"

He stared at her, and lifted his hands, palms up. "I'm not arguing with anyone."

"I heard you!"

He opened up his top desk drawer and took out a tape recorder. "I was dictating. That is all."

"You're lying!" She strode over to the desk and slammed her hands against it. "Stop it! You're lying to me, and you're hiding things from me, and you have no right to do so!"

He stood, a puzzled frown creasing his brow. "Madame Kiernan, I'm sorry. Please—"

"No!" Carly cried out. She hated this more than his anger or his cynicism or his mockery. She hated it when he created a total wall and behaved as if they barely knew each other. "Don't! Just—don't!"

She spun around and left him. He called after her, but she ran through the terrace and up the stairs and locked herself into her room.

He was making her insane.

She had heard voices. Two voices. No, he had been dictating.

Like hell! He had been arguing.

With himself?

With a disgusted oath of exasperation, Carly threw herself across the bed. She wished desperately that she had taken French at Columbia, instead of her two years of German. If she had only been able to pick out a few words of what had been said!

Frustrated, she changed for bed. She was about to turn off the light when she heard footsteps in the hall. Her heartbeat quickened. It was Jon, and he was coming to her. He would cast aside his bitter wall of defense and hold her again. And she would believe in him. No matter what.

There was a rap upon a door, but not hers.

Across the hall Tanya's door opened.

Carly heard Tanya laugh. "There you are! Come in, quickly!" Tanya's whisper was soft but throaty, and Carly strained to hear more. She could not.

She rushed across the room to her door and threw it open, but the door to Tanya's room had already closed.

"Damn!"

It occurred to her that she could just ask Tanya in the morning if she was having an affair with someone— Carly was certain that Tanya would certainly be blunt enough to ask her, if their roles had been reversed.

She lay in bed and, despite herself, enviously wondered whom Tanya was meeting. She lay there, awake and restless, and replayed the facts in her mind. People had been murdered. Jon could have committed the acts. She herself might very well have died that first night, when her coachman had been murdered.

Jasmine had disappeared. Her own sister.

Jon denied ever having had an affair with Jasmine. Geoffrey and Tanya had more than hinted that Jon and Jasmine had been involved.

And Carly still wanted him. She had sat there during dinner, and every time he had looked her way she had grown warm. When his fingers had brushed her flesh, when his breath had whispered over her nape, she had nearly cried out with the pain of wanting him....

At last she slept, restlessly.

At some point, as she struggled toward wakefulness, Carly became convinced that he was there with her. She breathed the subtle scent of his after-shave. If she just opened her eyes, he would be there; she would catch him.

If he was real.

She opened her eyes, and she was alone. "Damn you!" she cried softly to the darkness, tears stinging her eyes. She didn't know whether she had been more afraid that he would be there or that he would not. He was not mist; he could not come and go so easily.

But the scent of him lingered. It made her hurt worse, ache with a churning that twisted deep inside her.

She was afraid to get up. She didn't want to go to the balcony and see a silver wolf disappearing.

She didn't move, but stayed in bed, shivering. At last she began to doze again. As she drifted off to sleep, something bothered her. Something that she couldn't quite put her finger on. It was the scent, she thought. That after-shave, which was pleasant and stirring, with undertones that were so integral to him. There was something about him, something about the cologne. Something...

She just about had her finger on it. But she drifted off to sleep and it was lost to her. She tried to wake herself again, tried to remember, but the urge to sleep was too powerful.

In the morning she paced the floor, trying to remember. As she strode back and forth, a glimmer of pink dawn light reflected off something in the carpeting.

She paused and stooped. Her breath caught in her throat, she knelt and carefully extracted a loop diamond earring that was caught in the rose carpet.

She fingered it for a long time.

It was Jasmine's earring.

Carly held the piece of jewelry tightly in her fingers. Fear rose within her, and she closed her eyes as she swallowed and prayed desperately. Please, God, let Jasmine be all right!

She was still dressed in her flannel nightgown, with her hair all tangled but she rushed out of her room, anyway. She glanced at Tanya's door. She couldn't believe that Tanya's nocturnal visitor was Jon. She couldn't believe that he was a murderer—and she refused to believe that he would turn so quickly from her to another woman.

She crossed the hallway to the western side of the castle, where Jon Vadim's room was. She didn't give a damn if he was sleeping or not, and slammed a fist against his door.

There was no answer. Her heart thudded in her chest, and she told herself that she was a pathetic fool. Perhaps he was in Tanya's room, after all.

But then the door flew open. She had obviously awakened him, for his hair was tousled, and he looked irritated. He stared at her as he tied the belt of his robe.

"You again," he said.

She burst into the room, pacing on her bare feet in front of his bed.

"Jasmine is here."

"Jasmine is not here."

She paused and walked over to him, dangling the earring beneath his nose.

"This is Jasmine's!"

He reached for the earring. She clutched it in her fist, backing away from him.

"Give it to me." He started walking toward her.

"No! It is my sister's earring."

He stopped and shrugged. "*Oui.* Yes. It is Jasmine's earring. I've seen her wear it many times. But so what? Jasmine has been here often. Where did you find it?"

"In the rug."

"*Voilà.* You see." With the laissez-faire of a typical Frenchman, he shrugged again. "She lost her earring before she left. You have found it."

"I should have seen it before," she said.

"But you didn't."

"You're lying!" She realized her voice was rising hysterically. She was frightened and shaken and angry. And once again she didn't know how to feel or what to think.

"I am not lying to you! Jasmine must have lost it when—"

"She must have lost it recently. I would have found it before if it had been there."

He threw up his hands in disgust. "As you wish! You seem to have thought before that I did away with your sister. Perhaps I hid her in the dungeon. But now she was alive enough to come back and sneak into your room. And sneak back out. And not bother to tell her loving sister that she was back. *S'il vous plaît!* Madame Kiernan." He took a step toward her.

What he said was true, she conceded. Or was it? She didn't know anymore.

"Come here, please," he said to her.

She didn't want to listen to him. She wanted to think. "No! No!"

"I swear to you that Jasmine—"

"No! Don't swear to me anymore at all. I don't want to hear any more of it!"

"Please—"

"No! I'm leaving here this morning. I'm going to the hotel, and you are not going to stop me."

She turned and fled. She stormed into her room and tossed her suitcase onto the bed.

The door suddenly burst open. Startled, Carly swung around.

Jon was standing there. Briefly she marveled at the speed with which he had dressed. He was in dark jeans and riding boots and a red V-necked sweater.

"What do you think you're doing?" he asked her harshly.

"Packing," Carly told him curtly.

He strode on into the room. For a moment he watched her quick, angry strides from the dresser to the bed.

"Carly, stop it."

She did stop, just long enough to stare at him with a tempestuous and near-lethal fury. Then she started for the dresser again.

"Carly!" He caught her arm, and she was forced to stop. She was shaking badly, she realized. She didn't want to lose her dignity now. She stared at the hand that held her, at the bronze fingers that were curled over the soft flannel of her gown. He wasn't intimidated. He did not release her.

"Count Vadim," she said. "I would greatly appreciate it if you would take your—paw—off me."

"Paw? I see. I am part beast, and I attack people and use torture against them."

"Do you?" she inquired bluntly.

He didn't answer for a moment. He glared at her with a look of contempt. "No."

She tried to pull away. He held fast to her. "Count Vadim—"

"Stop calling me that."

"It's your name, isn't it?"

"You're not being reasonable."

"And you are?"

"I'm trying to talk to you."

"Well, I've tried and tried to talk to you. And now I don't want to talk anymore. I want to leave."

His mouth tightened. "You want to leave?" he asked harshly.

"Yes."

"Fine. That's just fine. We'll leave together."

"What—" Carly began. But she choked off her angry, indignant question as he pulled her roughly against him, sweeping his arm beneath her to lift her off her feet. Startled, she stared down into his eyes. They glittered with the sharp edge of his temper and determination. "Vadim, you can't do this—"

"But I can, Ms. Kiernan. I bloody well can, and I will."

He started walking so abruptly that she fell against him and instinctively hooked her arms around his neck. "What are you doing? Where are you taking me? You can't do this!"

But he was proving that he could. His strides brought them very quickly from the bedroom to the hallway and down the stairs. There was a maid on the terrace. Jon ignored her.

"I'm going to scream bloody murder!" Carly warned him.

"Enjoy yourself."

She gasped for breath, but didn't scream, though she didn't know why. He kept on striding across the courtyard. Satan was there, all saddled.

"What are you doing?" Carly demanded in exasperation. "I'm not even dressed!"

He almost smiled then. His eyes flickered over her as his arms tightened.

"You're perfect for what I've got in mind."

"What!"

He laughed. The next thing she knew, he'd hiked her over Satan's back, and leaped up behind her. Satan snorted and pranced. Carly swallowed a gasp of fear as the stallion reared and she fell back against Jon once more. His arms came around her to take hold of the reins. Satan set out across the cobblestones at a wild gallop.

"Where are we going?" Carly cried.

"To the devil, so it seems!" he retorted. "To the very devil!"

Her teeth chattering, Carly clung to the pommel. They entered the woods, and she thought she should be frightened. She wasn't. The tempest still raced through her. Mist rose from the ground, and she knew that wherever he took her, a storm would rage, for that sweet, rough magic was erupting again, all around the two of them and around the magnificent black horse that was bearing them toward their destiny.

Chapter 8

It was morning, and it was beautiful. The fall colors remained, flashing by them in a riot of splendor. Carly was alternately frightened and furious and then swept away. She couldn't believe his audacity, that he would dare to carry her away from his own home so openly, with such determination. Her temper skyrocketed, but there was more to it, too, a side she didn't want to admit. The scent of morning was glorious, the colors were splendid, and the rich, full fragrance of the earth was wonderful and heady. The morning was alive with freshness, with the sweet dampness of dew, with the excitement of the new day. It all seemed to fill her with a burst of hot, racing adrenaline, and she was achingly aware of his touch, of the wall of his chest behind her and the feeling of his arms around her. The horse moved beneath them with rugged and fluid power, and the air tore about them. She was angry; she was even still frightened.

But nothing like this could ever have happened in Manhattan.

She didn't know where the mad ride was leading them; he never had any doubts. Time passed and the wind and the colors whipped by them. They came at last to the cottage in the woods, the hunter's cottage where he had brought her that very first night, where he had first kissed her. Where she had admitted to herself that there was so much hypnotism in his kiss that he could have taken it wherever, whenever he chose, when they were mere strangers.

They weren't strangers any longer. They were adversaries, perhaps, but lovers, too, and she could not forget that. Not that he intended to let her.

"Whoa, Satan," he said, and slipped from the animal's back, letting the reins trail. He reached up for Carly, and she fought to remind herself that Jasmine was still missing, that nothing had changed. That he'd really had no right to bring her here. That she was a fool to love a man so blindly.

"Come here." He seemed to growl out the words. She stared down at him. His windswept hair lay across his forehead, and his eyes carried the windswept fever of their brisk ride. He was ready for battle.

"Who do you think you are, Count Vadim?" she asked him coolly. But she was feeling reckless and bold, and she knew she was quite ready to enter into the fray herself.

"Come down," he said.

"I won't."

"You will."

"I won't."

"This is ridiculous!" he exclaimed, exploding. His hands encircled her waist, and he dragged her down before him. She slid against his body, her nightgown caught against his belt buckle and her bare limbs entwined themselves with his. He was tense. His leg muscles were rock hard, and the soft flesh of her bare belly was touched by the pressure of his hips and the swelling rise within his jeans. She was so sensitive to his touch that her breath caught and she was stunned into a momentary silence. He allowed her to continue to slide against him as his hands spanned the silky flesh over her hips.

She realized dimly that since he'd first touched her, a part of her had thought of nothing else except being held by him again. She had yearned for the feeling of his lips, his hands. She had ached for his touch, inside and out, and at this moment, as she met the golden electrical storm in his eyes, she felt desire snake into her in a hot fury. She wondered whether this could be Carly Kiernan, reserved, logical, intelligent and wary. He had spoken to her of hunger, and she had learned what it meant. Fear still edged her heart, but the need, the desperate, searing ache, was greater than anything she had ever known.

His arms encircled her neck. She tried to keep her distance, but he laced his fingers at the small of her back and pressed her to him. And still, her voice quavering, she tried to talk. She tried to cling to the anger and deny the desire. "This is hideous behavior."

"Hideous behavior?" he queried.

"Adolescent! Macho."

"Oh, do you think so?"

"Definitely! After you lie—"

"I've never lied to you!"

"Then you evade the damn truth!"

"You ask too many questions."

"Because you lie—"

"I don't lie! I told you that. Not in anything that matters."

"So you do lie—"

"I didn't say that!"

"Then what are you saying?"

"I'm saying that you're a spoiled little brat. When the going is easy, you're all for it. Throw in a little trouble—"

"A little trouble!" She realized she was shouting. She was barefoot and shouting and trembling. She wanted to slam her fists against him until she rocked the truth from him. "My sister is missing, and people are dead—"

"And you turned on me. Right away. You acted as if things between us mattered, then you turned on me."

"Oh!" she exclaimed in exasperation, slamming her fists against him. He caught her and wrenched her close.

"Stop it! I've got you here now, and so help me, you're going to trust me."

"Trust you! After this? You have no right. You have no right whatever to act like this! To force people to your will. To drag a woman off as if you were still living in a cave. You have no right."

"I don't?"

"No."

"Oh, the hell I don't!" he shouted, and kissed her. Hard. Forcefully. He kissed her as if the thought of melding their lips had been with him forever, haunting him to the point of desperation. He molded her body to his and let his hands roam freely over her back and through her hair, and the unleashed fever in him erupted in her. Hot fire leaped and careened through her. She could scarcely breathe, yet neither could she tire of that kiss as it deepened and blossomed. It sowed its seeds deep inside her; its rugged passion filled her mouth, engaged her tongue, then was taken from her. He raked his teeth lightly over her lower lip, and then his mouth claimed hers all over again. Then his lips, just as fervent, just as wild, fell on her throat, and she gasped in abandon, arching her neck in response to his sensual assault.

He lifted her off her feet and, holding her close, carried her into the cottage.

"I had to get you away," he said.

"Yes."

"Things were going too far. I couldn't bear to see you and not touch you."

"I know."

The door fell shut behind them. He lowered her to the bunk. Their lips met, then they looked each other in the eye.

"I couldn't bear the fear in your eyes," he told her.

"I know you couldn't—do such things."

"I had to sit at dinner and look at your hair sweeping over your shoulders. I wanted to stand up and scream and rip you out of your chair and press my lips against your throat and taste your flesh."

"At dinner?"

"At dinner."

She smiled as he stretched himself beside her. "We're not at dinner anymore. What's stopping you?"

"That ridiculous flannel gown."

"It isn't ridiculous!"

"It is when you're longing to kiss a woman's shoulders." His smile was the rueful smile of an enchanting rogue. His eyes held hers while he slipped a hand to the hemline of her gown. His fingers grazed her calves and knees and traveled along her inner thigh, then curved around one hip. He pressed his lips against the curve of her hip, then, impatient, he tugged at the gown, pulling her to him. He buried his head against her shoulder, tossing the offending flannel onto the floor, and the pressure of his mouth sent hot new sensations rushing through her. She dug her fingers into his hair, holding him close. She trembled fiercely and felt the furious thunder of his heart against her breast.

She slipped her hands into his waistband, dragging his sweater upward. In seconds she had cast it on top of her gown on the floor. She stroked the length of his back and lightly bit the hard muscles of his shoulders, moving her breasts against the coarse hair and hardness of his chest.

He let out a harsh oath and pulled away from her to scramble out of his boots and socks and jeans and briefs. She watched him with growing anticipation and restless urgency, then closed her arms around him gratefully when he returned to her. She felt the fever of his body and the male power, and she was desperately eager for him, yet he suddenly held back. He rose above her and grazed her cheek with the back of his knuckles.

His voice was harsh and hard as he said, "You can't be afraid of me."

"I'm not afraid of you."

Now he was aggressive, fierce in his passion. His touch was no longer gentle as he threaded his fingers into her hair. "You have to believe in me."

"I do." It wasn't a lie. When she stared into his glowing amber eyes, she could think of nothing but him. Doubts and suspicion and uncertainty fled.

He lowered his voice, rumbling like the thunder of the storm. It was as tense and passionate as his hold upon her. "You have to want me."

"I do."

"You have to be—hungry."

"I am," she whispered. She smiled, because she wasn't afraid in the least. Not of the strength in his hands, not of his temper, not of his arrogance or ferocity, his past or his future. She didn't mind the tension in his fingers or the trembling in his body. She stroked his cheek and allowed her fingers to travel down his body as he held his weight over her. She stroked the furrow of hair down to his waist and past it, over the hard contour of his belly and beyond. Staring at him, at his fever, at his tension, she felt curiously at peace— and ragingly alive. She felt wonderfully wicked and mischievous . . . and pure, because she was really very much in love with him, she realized. Blindly in love, maybe. But deeply, desperately so. She loved the sheen on his brow and the rigid constriction of his sinewy body. Still he held himself away from her. She wouldn't allow it. She feathered her fingers over him to taunt and curled them around him with purpose.

She felt the spasm as he jerked. She marveled sweetly at her power as he shuddered and convulsed. "I am hungry," she promised him, her eyes innocently wide in her seduction. "Hungry as a silver-gray wolf . . ."

He emitted some hoarse cry and caught her hand. With a sudden movement he wedged his knees between her thighs, cast back his head and, grinding his teeth, entered her swiftly. There was no more finesse, no more play, just the throbbing burst of passion. He sank like a blade into a velvet liner until her body absorbed the shock, then he gave free vent to the frustration of the days that had elapsed between them. She clung to him and rode the storm, though she had never known anything like it. He enveloped her body with his, cried out again, and while he moved in a frantic, sweeping beat, he tugged her nipple into his mouth, and chords of passion rippled through her. She undulated to meet him and dug her fingers into his shoulders, let them drift over the small of his back, then with soaring abandon gripped the tight muscles of his buttocks. Sensations surged like a growing drumbeat, harder and harder, and then burst, showering her in the liquid warmth of his body and leaving her with a delicious lethargy that barely left her the strength to whisper his name as he fell against her.

They lay there, silent, unmoving, just touching, and feeling the rise and fall of their chests as they fought for a normal flow of breath. Their bodies began to cool at last. The air danced around them, chilling, fall air.

Carly shivered. Jon rose quickly, stripped the blanket from beneath them and wrapped it around her. Naked, he walked over to the fireplace and hunkered down to set another piece of wood on the grate and kindling above it. He lit the kindling with a long match and then waited, watching the flame take. Satisfied, he rose. He strode over to one of the cabinets and slammed through them until he found another blanket. He wrapped it around his shoulders, then found a coffeepot and a foil bag of coffee. Carly watched him in silence. She was growing cold, yet she was delighted, for she still felt a part of him. She tried to tell herself that he was a passionate man; he would love any woman so deeply. She didn't want to accept such an idea, so she didn't. She hugged herself and cherished the quivering that remained inside her, the inner warmth that had seeped from his body into hers. She felt very intimate with him. Whatever he was, she longed to remain a part of him.

"This will take a minute," he said to her.

She nodded. She was still shivering. Smiling, he came back to her and lifted her in his arms, blanket and all. He brought her before the fire, and they sank together before the growing golden warmth. He smoothed back her hair and stroked her face. "Better?"

"Yes."

"If you want me to apologize, I really can't," he told her stiffly.

Carly smiled and kept her eyes lowered. "I don't want you to apologize."

"No?"

"No."

He moved her face into his left arm and lifted her chin with his right hand. He searched her eyes and brushed his lips over hers. It was his first real expression of tenderness that day. The other had been exquisite and excruciating and something they had fervently needed. She cherished the explosiveness of need, marveling at her own. But she adored the tenderness, too, and was startled to find she had to blink to hide a sudden surge of tears.

"I love you, you know," he told her. It was almost a casual remark.

Her heart quickened. "Do you?" she whispered. "Can you—really?"

"I do, and I can."

She cradled his clean-shaven chin. "I love you, too."

"I like the way you show it," he said brusquely.

"Me! I didn't drag you out in your nightwear—"

"Well, since I sleep naked, we would have gotten a few stares."

She started to giggle, but then she recalled that he hadn't been naked that morning. She had seen pajama legs beneath his robe.

"Carly, what is it?"

"If you would just quit behaving so strangely!"

"What?" There was a new note in his voice, and his arm tightened.

She didn't answer him right away, and he questioned her again. "What are you talking about?"

"This morning."

"Oh." He was silent for a moment. "Well, I'm sorry. Oh, not for dragging you out here. It was my only chance. You were trying to leave, and I couldn't let you do that. I'm sorry for—whatever I did this morning."

She moved from him, staring into the fire. He reached for her and pulled her back. "Carly! I said I'm sorry."

She swung around. "Yes, yes! Fine, but you're frightening me! Don't you remember?"

"I was—er—half asleep."

"Half asleep? You came after me like gangbusters."

"Yes, well, I was desperate then. I knew you were angry."

He didn't let her reply. He rose and went back toward the rustic stove where the coffee was perking. He found two mugs and poured out coffee. "I hope you can take it black. I have sugar but no cream here."

"It's warm. I'll take it any way that I can get it," Carly replied.

Jon came back with the coffee. He sat down beside her, offering her a mug. She sipped it, nearly burning her lips. His arm encircled her once more, and she relaxed against it. "Why were you so angry with me?" she murmured.

He sighed, rubbing his chin on the top of her head, then taking a long swallow of the hot coffee. "I just thought that you were seeing me as some heinous criminal every time that you looked at me. And then Alexi irritated me, I suppose. His family is as old as mine—we were just richer and more powerful. But I promise you—he has a few skeletons in his basement, too. They were medieval landlords, our ancestors. Hell, you Americans still have capital punishment."

"I never imagined you taking a whip and chain to anyone," Carly told him innocently.

"And I never will," he teased her in reply, "just as long as you behave."

"Jon!"

He laughed and hugged her. "I'm sorry. I couldn't resist, though I suppose I should. Under the circumstances."

Carly was silent for a long moment. She swallowed the last of her coffee, then swung on him with determination. "Jon, I do love you, and I believe in you, but you are lying to me."

"Carly—"

She pressed her fingers against his lips. "You are. You're lying, or you're evading the truth. There are things that you aren't telling me."

He caught her hand, curled his fingers around it and held it close to his heart. His eyes seared earnestly into hers. "Carly, if there is anything that I'm not telling you, it's because others are involved. Because I could create more danger. I wouldn't hurt you in any way if I could prevent it. Can you believe that?"

She hesitated, but not for long. The same magic that she had felt from the start was stealing over her. When he looked at her like that, she felt her will slip away.

Was it hypnotism, or was it love? she wondered. Were they, perhaps, one and the same?

"Carly?" He tightened his fingers around hers. His eyes were golden fire, burning and consuming, lapping against any pretense she might have made of denial. "It won't be long," he promised. "Believe in me. Believe that I love you."

She tore her eyes from his and stared at the flames that had taken hold in the hearth and were now burning high. "I wish I could see my sister."

"I swear to you, Jasmine is safe."

"She was afraid. She begged me to come."

"She is safe. I'm certain of it. Honestly."

Carly stared back at him. She smiled ruefully. "Everyone implies that you and she were very involved. You deny it."

"Yes. I deny it heartily. Whatever you hear, it isn't the truth. I have never been anything more than a friend to Jasmine."

She believed him. She wanted to believe him. No man could speak so sincerely and not be telling the truth. Setting down her cup she leaned forward, and drew an idle pattern on the floor with her forefinger. "Things are so strange here."

Watching her, he grinned. The blanket was slipping from her shoulders, and he thought he had never seen a more perfect woman in his life. Her breasts were firm and full and high, and they peeped out from the blanket with wide, rouge-crested peaks, setting his adrenaline flowing again. She was delicately built, with smooth ivory skin that was silk to his touch. Her breasts and shoulders tapered to a slim waist, and beneath it her hips flared out again, fascinating and feminine. Her face was shaped like a heart, with high cheekbones that could give her a cool arrogance to rise above any occasion. Her eyes were the color of a tropical sea. Everything about her was feminine and sexually appealing, and yet part of the great fascination she held for him was in the steady determination and intelligence in those beautiful eyes, wonderful eyes that were wiser than time. And then he was in love with her hair, too. Gold like the sun, like honey, like a field of rippling wheat.

He reached out and pushed the blanket from her shoulders. Surprised, she turned to him, but he knew the newly risen passion in his gaze must have been very evident. He shrugged the blanket off his own shoulders and rose to his knees before her. He reached out with both hands, cupped her breasts and moved his fingers over the crests again and again. She gasped and rose to her knees, too, planting her hands against his shoulders. He leaned to kiss the pulse at the base of her throat, and she tilted her head to give him free access. He drew her hard against him and availed himself of her breasts, groaning as he tasted the sweet salt of her body and savored the feeling of her nipple against his tongue, in his mouth. He moved his hands down her body and between her legs. He stroked her thighs and ventured higher, and his whole body tensed and tightened and became fully aroused when he rubbed his thumb against her. She moaned against his shoulder, and he captured her lips and then lifted her high above him and brought her back down. She took him into herself slowly, straddled over him, smiling with shy pleasure. Then a strand of gold fell over her eyes and she shuddered, and he cupped her buttocks and she began to move against him.

He'd never known a woman who could do what she did to him. Just watching her, he became unbearably aroused. He dreamed of her by night, ached for her by day. She rocked against him with shuddering pleasure, and the sensations were wonderful and wildly explosive. He held her, he touched her, he guided her. He swept his hands around her breasts, then cradled her derriere, urging her ever more fiercely against him. He marveled at the beauty in her eyes, at the openness of her passion, and even as the splendor burst in upon him he began to pray that he wouldn't lose her when she learned the truth.

She fell against him. Ruffling her hair, he whispered to her in guttural tones what she had just done for him, and added with tenderness just how much he loved her. He held her close and prayed again.

It wasn't that he was lying; he was evading the truth. Or maybe he was lying, because nothing about him was real. Nothing but his feelings for her.

She lay against him. The fire touched her face and lit up her hair. It sent a bronze cast over the sleek, shimmering beauty of her breasts. She smiled at him, and his heart pounded inside his chest. He stood up, sweeping her along with him. Raising a brow to him in question, she wrapped her arms around him with complete trust.

"The floor got hard," he explained.

"Oh," she said simply. "I could have walked."

"Yes, but I suppose I'm just plain macho and all those other things you called me."

She was silent.

"You're not denying anything," he told her gruffly. He let her down a little hard on the bed, then crawled up beside her.

She smiled, threading her fingers through his hair. "What's to deny?"

"You're still mad."

"It was horrible behavior."

"It was not," he said.

"But I will forgive you this time. Because..."

"Because what?"

She rolled over on her stomach, trailing her fingers over the hair on his chest. "Well, it was obnoxious. But well..."

"Well, what, damn it?"

"I suppose it had its romantic elements, too."

"Hmph," he muttered. She smiled and laid her cheek on the pillow. He put his arm around her. In a few minutes he realized that she had dozed off. He closed his eyes and slept.

Carly woke first. She didn't move, just stared at him and appreciated all the fine little things about him. She liked his nose. It was what they called a Roman nose, she supposed. His brow was fine and wide. His hair was as dark as the night, and it fell over his forehead and his eyes in an enchanting way when he slept. She liked his chest. He had wonderful broad shoulders and taut muscles, and she loved the short, crisp flurry of dark hair on his chest that tapered in a line to his navel, and flared out again below his hips.

She realized that his eyes were open now and that he was surveying her in turn. He stroked her hair. "What happened to your husband, Carly? Jasmine said once that he was very ill."

"Cancer," she said softly.

"It must have been very painful."

"He was one of the bravest people I ever knew." And he had been. He had known that he was dying, but he had never complained about his treatments. His only concern had been his life insurance, because he was old-fashioned and had worried about her when he was gone.

"You must have loved him very much," Jon murmured.

"I did." She propped herself up on an elbow and smiled at him ruefully. "I will always love him. But I love you...too. I really do. So fiercely. It's different. Do you understand that?"

He swallowed. She was so honest with him, he thought. She had opened her heart.

And he was living a lie.

"I understand completely," he replied. "You should always love him, Carly. That doesn't take anything away from us."

She picked up his hand and kissed his fingertips. "Nothing can be taken away from us," she promised him with sweet passion.

He closed his eyes, praying that what she said was so. When he opened his eyes again, he stared at her with all the heat and fever of his emotion gleaming in his gaze. He clutched her shoulders tightly, barely realizing his force. "I do love you. Remember that. I do love you."

She didn't protest his ferocity. She kissed him, slowly, sweetly. "I believe you."

He released her quickly, ruefully, realizing that he was hurting her. "I'm sorry. I just want you to remember that."

"Why?"

"Because— Carly, you just have to trust me for now. There are things happening here that you don't know about, that you can't possibly understand. And I'm not involved alone."

She listened to him and nodded, then sprang out of bed, naked. He lay back, somewhat awed, glad that she could feel so uninhibited and natural with him.

"I'm starving," she said. "Is there anything to eat here?"

"There should be something." He tossed the blankets aside and stood up to join her.

They dug through the cabinets together and found crackers and an assortment of cheeses. Jon found a hard roll of German summer sausage, and they brought the cache back to the bed with them. They ate, spreading different cheeses for each other and dropping tidbits of food into each other's mouths.

Then Jon looked at her in that way again, his eyes glowing gold, filled with tension. He cleared the bed of food and fell on top of her, avidly kissing her, sweeping his tongue over her, devouring her as if she were a necessity of life. Gasping with wonder, she quickly joined him in breathless passion, amazed that it could grow even headier, ever more fervent. With his touch, his kiss, he roamed the length of her, doing things that were achingly intimate. He brought her to the brink of ecstasy, then he forced her over the brink and began all over again, coming to her, filling her.

She slept again and then was stunned to realize that it was dark outside and that they had spent the whole day in the cottage, doing nothing but make love.

"We should go back," she murmured.

He threw one arm over his eyes and answered lazily, "I don't ever want to go back."

Grinning, Carly found her flannel nightgown and threw his jeans none too gently at his replete and outstretched body. "At least you have clothing to go back in!" she chastised him.

He grinned. "Everyone—and I do mean everyone—will know exactly what we've been up to all day."

"And you don't care."

"I don't give a bloody damn. I'm in love."

She laughed. She slipped back into her gown, but couldn't help chiding him one more time. "Mr. Macho! You do what you will, take what you want, and whoever might not like it can go to the devil."

He grinned. "I feel just like Tarzan. I'd love to beat my fists against my breast in triumph."

In return, Carly sniffed. He laughed and rose, sweeping her against him. He kissed her, then regretfully released her. "I guess we do have to get back." He stepped into his jeans and zipped them up.

Carly said, "This is going to be awkward for me. At seven o'clock at night, I'm going to reappear in a flannel nightgown."

"What will people think?" Jon teased her.

"Well, Tanya shouldn't think anything," Carly mused. "She has a man in her room almost every night."

"What?"

Jon spun on her so suddenly that she nearly jumped. He was rigid, she saw, and dead serious.

"She—she meets someone," Carly said.

"You've seen him?" Jon demanded.

"No," Carly said, troubled. She hugged her knees, watching him. "I thought at first that it might be you."

He pulled his sweater over his head. She guessed that he was taking the time to regain his composure.

"No, it's not me," he said. "And you know that." He paused, frowning. "You do know that, don't you?"

She smiled. "Yes."

He sat on the foot of the bed to put on his socks and boots. "But you don't know who it is?" he asked her slowly, not looking her way. "Not at all? I mean, is it one of the servants or Geoffrey or Alexi—or who?"

"I have no idea," Carly said. "Why? Why is it so important?"

"Oh, it's not. I'm just curious. I wonder why she and this man—whoever he is—would want to hide an affair."

Carly shrugged. She didn't know and didn't care. As long as the man wasn't Jon.

"The earring bothers me," she murmured.

"What earring?"

"Jasmine's earring."

He smiled, shaking his head ruefully, "Carly, what are you talking about?"

She straightened, looking at him reproachfully. "I swear, sometimes I think that you're trying to make me insane. You run hot and cold, fire and ice. The earring. I told you about it this morning."

He looked down at his boot. "I'm sorry. I don't remember."

Carly frowned. That icy little finger of doubt and fear was scratching at her heart again. "We had a fight about it. That's why I almost left. That was why you trailed after me. That's why…today," she said lamely.

He sat down beside her. He pressed his temples with his palms, then shook his head. "Carly, I'm sorry. Bear with me, please. What is this about the earring?"

"I found Jasmine's earring in the carpet."

"Well, Jasmine has been at the castle. Recently."

She shook her head. Was he losing his mind, or was she losing hers? "I know that. But how come I didn't see the earring before?"

"Maybe it isn't even Jasmine's," he said. But she was certain that he was concerned, and puzzled, too.

"No, I'd know the earring anywhere," she replied. "It was a present from Dad. There can be only two of them in the world, I'm certain."

He rose but didn't face her. "Well, then, she must have lost it before. And you just didn't notice it."

Carly wondered if he himself believed what he said, yet she was certain that if Jasmine had been near, he would be just as surprised as she.

"Let's go back," he told her, reaching out to her. He pulled her close and kissed her again, long and passionately. "I don't ever want to forget this day," he said. "I want to cherish it forever."

"Yes...." she whispered.

"Even though you spent it with a manhandling, manipulative caveman?"

"It sounds much worse with an English accent," Carly told him.

He laughed and went over to kill the fire. Satisfied, he caught her hand. He threw open the door, and the night came in upon them, dark and misty. And dangerous.

"Satan!" Jon called. "Where are you?"

They heard a loud snort. Satan, with a mouthful of grass, ambled over to them. "Well, thank goodness you stayed around this afternoon," Jon told the animal affectionately.

Carly was amazed that the stallion could be so well behaved. She smiled ruefully with sudden doubt. "He ran off on Halloween," she reminded him.

"Yes, he did, didn't he."

"And he's such a well-mannered horse. He wasn't tied all day, and he's still right here, ready and waiting."

"Some days are better than others."

"You know what I think?"

"What?" Jon grinned. He lifted her up, setting her upon the horse's back.

"I think you let him run away on purpose."

"Do you think that I would do such a thing?" He mounted behind her.

"Yes," Carly said bluntly.

"Well, maybe."

"So you admit it?"

"I don't admit a thing," he said.

She leaned against him as they rode along. "And then there's that wolf...."

It seemed that his arms tightened around her and that he waited expectantly. "Yes?" he murmured, and she detected a wary note in his voice.

The wolf, the silver-gray timber wolf, she recalled. She had feared he meant to consume her on Halloween. But then he and Jon had been there with her together, and they had seemed to blend into one. When the one disappeared, the other seemed to appear.

"Never mind," she said. It was just too ludicrous.

"Hold tight," he told her.

Satan moved swiftly through the mist. In the darkness Carly could see Castle Vadim high above them, grim and foreboding and hauntingly gothic. The lights were on, lights that should have promised warmth.

They clattered back into the courtyard. It was almost dinnertime. Geoffrey, Alexi and Tanya, all dressed to the hilt, were already on the terrace, watching as Satan stopped in the courtyard.

Carly decided she just had to brave it out. She slid down from the horse without Jon's help. "That was really a beautiful ride. Thank you," she told him. She met Tanya's wide eyes. "Oh, are we really that late? I'll dress quickly." No one said anything. She offered them all a sweeping smile and hurried up the stairs.

She was in love. When she closed the door behind her, she burst into laughter and realized that she was already dreaming of the night to come.

She bathed and dressed with special care, because she was euphoric and dreamed of meeting him again that night. She longed to sleep beside him in a comfortable bed. She longed to feel his warmth through the night. She longed for him to waken and want to make love.

She wore a black velvet sheath dress with a string of pearls and let her hair fall over her shoulders. At dinner, she chatted with Geoffrey about the play, and laughed with Alexi over the region's superstitions. She met Tanya's openly curious stare with a shrug and waited for Jon to appear.

She and Jon laughed together so easily that evening, sitting by each other. Their knees brushed, and he held her fingers and kissed her often. He was devastating, she reflected. Black was his color. He was rugged and masculine and elegant and sophisticated. She had never been happier than now, knowing that his golden gaze fell upon her and that his whisper was for her ears only.

His whisper . . . promising that he would come to her, that he would be with her by midnight.

She escaped the dinner table early. She wanted to change and brush her hair and freshen her cologne and await his arrival.

She still walked on clouds as she returned to her room. He would come to her. She was smiling when she opened and closed her door. In a fog she kicked off her high heels and unclasped her pearls. Then she saw the dark-haired woman in the middle of the room, the beautiful woman with the wealth of black curls and the huge sapphire-blue eyes.

"Jasmine!" Carly gasped.

"Shh!"

But they rushed for each other, hugging fiercely. Relief flooded through Carly. Jasmine was alive and well, and she was seeing her and touching her at last.

Carly pushed away from her sister. Uncharacteristically, Jasmine was wearing black jeans and a black turtleneck sweater.

"What in God's name are you up to?" Carly began severely. "You had me scared to death! You made me travel halfway across the world and worry myself silly."

"Stop, please!" Jasmine begged.

"Then give me some explanations. Quickly."

"Don't scold!" Jasmine protested sulkily. "And please, keep your voice down. You don't understand! I'm in danger! There are very strange things going on."

Carly hesitated, watching her sister worriedly. "I thought you'd been here. I found your earring today."

Jasmine smiled and touched her ear. "I hadn't even realized I'd lost it."

"But you were in here."

"Yes. Oh, it's a long story."

"Well?"

Jasmine took her hands earnestly. "Carly, we're in danger. We're really in danger."

Jasmine never had been able to tell a story from beginning to end, but as Carly looked into her luminous blue eyes she knew that her sister was really frightened.

"We have to tell the count—" Carly began.

"What!" Jasmine protested, shaking her head furiously. "Don't be ridiculous. That isn't Jon Vadim."

Carly felt as if a two-ton rock had slammed her in the face. "What?" she demanded sickly.

"That isn't Jon Vadim. That isn't the count. Carly—" Jasmine broke off, growing pale. "It's *him*!"

Carly nodded, unable to speak as Jon called, "Carly! Damn it, open this door. Are you all right? Carly, I'm coming in."

He would come in. She sensed it; she knew it. He would throw his shoulder against the wood and break the lock. Jon would do something like that.

Except that it wasn't Jon Vadim.

"Answer the door!" Jasmine pleaded. "He'll come in!"

Carly stared from her sister to the door. He was calling her again, and he sounded tense, worried.

She ran over to answer it. He had lied to her. He wasn't even Jon Vadim.

Who the hell was he? an inner voice screamed.

She ran to the door and turned around.

Jasmine had disappeared.

"Carly!" he yelled.

The door burst open.

Chapter 9

Carly could scarcely breathe. She didn't know whether to scream out, praying that someone would come to her rescue, or pretend that she didn't know the truth about Jon. That Jasmine hadn't just been in her room to tell her that the real and tangible man she had fallen in love with wasn't real at all. He was an impostor. He had asked her to trust him, and he was living some fabulous lie.

Jasmine had disappeared. Carly didn't know whether her sister was hiding beneath the bed, in the bathtub, or perhaps in the armoire. There hadn't been time for her to escape out the terrace windows. But Carly knew Jasmine must have been terrified to have run like that. Terrified of this man.

Carly wondered if he had murdered the real Count Vadim. Her heart pounding mercilessly, she stared into his amber wolf's eyes and wondered at the relentless power that lurked there. His hands were on his hips, and he seemed breathless himself. Keenly, swiftly, he scanned the room, then looked back at her. Still in his tux from dinner, he was striking and handsome and deadly, and she sensed the suspicion and danger and tension he emitted.

He was a night person, he had told her. He moved by night; he could see in the dark. Suddenly he seemed part of an evil world, a world where wolves preyed upon the unwary.

She had been very easy prey.

Carly stepped back. She blinked and suddenly realized that she couldn't tell him that Jasmine had been there. Jasmine had been afraid of him and was probably counting on her to steer him away, and quickly.

Where was her sister?

He ran his fingers through his hair, staring at her in sudden confusion. "Why the hell didn't you answer the door?"

Her first attempt at speech failed. She swallowed, and this time, words came out in a whisper, but heated and, at the last, indignant. "What do you think you're doing, breaking down the damned door?"

"What?" he demanded sharply. A moment's silence followed, and then he exploded. "Because I was scared to death, that's why! I called you and called you and called you, and you didn't answer. And you were supposed to be waiting for me."

"Oh," Carly said blankly.

His frown remained. She couldn't move; she felt paralyzed. An inner voice warned her that she must behave normally. She couldn't let him know what she knew. She had to give her sister the chance to escape.

"Carly! What's wrong?"

"Nothing," she said lamely. He took a step toward her and she took a step back. He narrowed his eyes and kept coming. "What the hell is the matter with you?"

"Nothing, I told you!"

He reached her, and she eluded him by leaping onto the bed and then over it. Breathing hard, she stared at him and realized sickly that she was making a fool of herself. A blind man would know that something was wrong. He clenched his jaw as he watched her, and he paused, hands on hips. He walked over to the door and did something with the knob. Carly heard a series of clicks. Then he turned back to her, leaning against the door. Handsome and casual, he gave her a cold grin that offered nothing in the way of humor.

"I didn't break it," he told her. He moved a hand to demonstrate the easy flow of the bolt. "We're locked in here now."

Carly nodded. He stood between her and the door. She could make a mad scramble for the balcony doors, she thought, but he would pounce on her in seconds flat. She just stood still, watching him.

He threw up his arms in disgust. "All right, Carly, come on. Game time is over. What the hell is wrong?"

She shook her head.

He started toward her slowly. There was really nowhere to run. She held her ground.

But he must have heard the echoing thunder of her heart. He must have seen the panic in her eyes and heard the desperate rasp of her breath. He stopped before her. He set his hand against her breast, and she nearly screamed. The touch tore into her, raw and scalding, and even with the truth before her, she wanted to deny it. She was in love with his scent, with how his eyes held her with their hypnotic gaze, and she ached for his touch as fiercely now as she ever had.

It was a lie. He was a lie, and everything he said or felt was a lie.

She wanted to scream, to demand to know who he was. Yet how could she? How could she do anything but allow her heart to pound and ice to weigh down her limbs as she wondered where Jasmine was, and prayed that he didn't find her.

"Your heart is beating like a jackhammer," he observed.

"Is it?"

His gaze grew rueful. "And it most definitely doesn't seem to be in anticipation of my arrival."

"You barged in on me."

"You were expecting me. You invited me. At least I think you did."

"I've—I've changed my mind."

"You've changed your mind."

"Yes!"

He closed his eyes, his hands still against her breast. She couldn't bear the touch and slid away from him. She tried to laugh, but despite herself the sound was uneasy. "I'm not in the mood, that's all."

He paused. Carly's knees grew weak, and she sank down on the foot of the bed. She felt a dizzying rush of blood come to her head. Jasmine must be hearing this conversation and wondering what lay between them. She must be sick over it.

He stood before her and wove his fingers through her hair, lifting her face to his.

"Not in the mood?" he inquired politely.

"All right, I'm sorry!" she snapped. "But I'm not! I—I've just decided that this is pointless, and I don't want it to go any further."

She wanted to look down, gaze away, do anything but feel his eyes boring into hers, feel the tension of his frame nearly touching her, feel the power of his fingers upon her.

Again he spoke to her. His voice was a husky whisper, low and sensual and lulling. "How can you forget? How can you change your mind? You said you loved me, and you showed me in every conceivable way that you did. I've never know a woman to give herself so freely, so...intimately."

Something about the sexuality of his voice spelled out almost every move they had made throughout the long day. Carly didn't know at that moment whether she was more frightened or mortified. The room spun. She wished he would move, for she didn't want to inhale his masculine scent. She didn't want him to use his fingers against her so, just lightly massaging her scalp, using a practiced tenderness against her.

"Please..." she said. "I have a headache."

"A headache?" he scoffed, almost laughing.

"Yes! A headache."

"Carly, please, you can be more original than that! And for an excuse like that, aren't you supposed to be married?"

"It's not an excuse. I have a headache. Believe me, I have a piercing headache. Please..." She tugged free from his hold and stared down at her hands. Why couldn't she wield more authority? Why the hell couldn't she get this man out of here?

At last, he started to walk away. She thought he was leaving her, but he was not. He headed for the bathroom. Carly panicked, wondering if Jasmine was in the shower. She leaped up, raced ahead of him and braced herself against the door. He stopped, smiling curiously, brows raised.

"What— Where are you— What are you doing?" she demanded.

"I was just going to wash my hands. I have a smudge of something on my knuckles from the door."

"Oh."

"May I pass?"

Had he killed the real Count Vadim? She trembled, and she couldn't believe it, but she suddenly saw an image of him striding in and sweeping back the shower curtain in a fury. He would find Jasmine standing there, and maybe he would curl his fingers about her throat, because he didn't dare have her around to tell the truth.

"No!" she cried.

"No—I can't pass?" he asked her.

She nodded. He would brush right by her any second, she was certain. Not really knowing what she was doing, she hurled herself toward him with a sudden burst of energy and landed in his arms. She threw her own around him and kissed him. She ran her fingers through his hair and pressed her breasts against his muscled chest.

He held her and returned the kiss, moving his hands down her back, bringing her higher against him, cupping her buttocks. Hot, searing sensations leaped into her and streaked back and forth. Their hips met and ground together. She fought for logic and reason, and tears stung her eyes, because she could still want him so desperately. He had lied to her with every word, but when he touched her he played her like a puppet, and she could not escape his power, the charisma of his kiss.

She was trying to make him forget his quest, she reminded herself. And with a chill in her heart she knew that she had loved him before, and that what had been must meld with what was now. If she touched him again, what difference would it make, for she had touched him so thoroughly before? She had to be with him. She had to let Jasmine escape.

He broke away from her, moving his thumbs over her throat and chin as he searched out her eyes. "What about your headache?"

"It's better. It's miraculously better."

"Hmm. I wonder if headaches disappear so easily for married couples," he mused skeptically. Then he added carefully, "I thought you weren't in the mood."

"What?" She gazed up at him. He kissed her throat, and she wondered if she would really care if he intended to slit her veins. She even wondered in some foggy corner of her mind if he wouldn't become a silver-gray wolf, right before her eyes, and tear into her heart, and soul and mind....

"I, er, I got back into the mood once my headache disappeared," she explained.

His lips touched her flesh. There was nothing but tenderness in his caress. He put his arms around her. She was floating, remembering that she loved him. Jasmine must be wrong. There couldn't be anything evil about this man, Carly knew; she loved him.

She moaned softly as she felt the mattress underneath her. She tangled her fingers in his hair and held him as he pressed kisses against her throat and collarbone and the lobe of her ear. She locked her fingers around his neck, meeting his kisses and returning them with sweet seduction.

Surely Jasmine would understand the sacrifice. She would slip from her hiding place and escape. She would have the sense to realize that Carly was covering for her.

"I love you," he whispered to her, his lips but an inch from hers.

Aching, she nodded. He loosened his tie, then drew it from his collar, staying close to her as he did so. Then he moved, and she watched through half-closed eyes as he shed his jacket. He turned again and headed for the bathroom.

His spell had been strong, she lay there for endless seconds before she realized that she had not seduced him—he had seduced and tricked her, and now he was on the prowl again. With a sharp cry she leaped to her feet and raced after him. He had already drawn back the shower curtain.

No one was in the tub.

"What are you doing now?" Carly demanded even as she breathed a sigh of relief. He didn't answer but cast her a withering glare and pushed past her to return to the bedroom. On his knees, he ripped at the bed coverings. Carly gasped, thinking, This is it! He will drag her out and we will both be at his mercy and he will know that we know....

"Don't, please! Don't! Wait—" she began, but he was tossing back the covering and glaring at her once more as he got to his feet.

Jasmine was not under the bed.

He strode over to the armoire. Carly knew that had to be it. Jasmine couldn't have disappeared into thin air. Carly couldn't let him find her sister.

"No!" she yelled, and pitched herself forward. She fell at his feet and wound her arms around his legs. He stared down at her, his golden gaze sharpened by disdain.

If Jasmine was all right, if they both lived through this, Carly decided, she would definitely kill her sister. "Don't, please..."

He reached down for her hands and dragged her back to her feet. "Stop it, Carly," he told her harshly. "By God, I am going to know what is going on." He pushed back the armoire's sliding doors. This time Carly swallowed her panic and terror and made no sound. Feeling her knees shake, she was afraid that they would give again.

"Damn!" he yelled.

Jasmine was not in the armoire.

"What are you doing?" Carly cried out as he headed for the balcony doors. He threw them open, and the cold night wind rushed in upon them. Carly shivered, but he seemed not to notice. He stepped out into the mist and the moonlight. The glow fell on the starched white of his shirt and the harsh planes of his handsome face. She barely dared to breathe a sigh of relief.

The balcony was empty. Somehow Jasmine had managed to disappear into thin air, so it seemed.

The man Carly had known as Jon Vadim moved back into the room. He stared at her with no tenderness. "What the hell is going on?"

"You're asking me?" she demanded, incredulous.

"Who were you talking to?" He strode toward her with menace.

This wasn't the lover she had known, not in any way, she thought.

"I wasn't talking to anyone!" She was frightened by his total ruthlessness. She cried out, evading him again, running. She had to run, but there was nowhere to go.

She went out to the balcony and gazed at the stones of the courtyard, far, far below. As she leaned over the ancient balustrade, gasping for breath, she closed her eyes and thanked God that Jasmine hadn't fallen.

Then her prayers ceased, for she realized that he was behind her, and that his arms were sweeping around her waist.

She opened her mouth to scream.

He clamped his hand down upon her, and she barely got out a whimper.

"Damn it to hell, Carly, what is the matter with you tonight?" Holding her mouth closed, he picked her up off her feet so that her toes dangled just off the floor. He whispered into her ear, "Do you hear me, *my love*?" There was a great deal of bitterness in the endearment.

Carly couldn't answer him; she could scarcely breathe.

"Do you hear me? Ah, hell!" he spat the words out in disgust. "I'm not trying to hurt you—"

She bit into his fingers with all the fear and vengeance that were high in her heart. He cried out savagely and eased his hold on her. But before she could draw breath for a new attempt at a scream, he wound his left hand around her. He pressed the injured fingers to his mouth and swore, then dragged her into the room single-handedly and secured the balcony doors.

"As I was saying to you," he hissed through gritted teeth, "I'm not trying to hurt you!"

He slammed her down onto the bed. Even as she tried to rise, he straddled her and with his palm pressed her lips against her teeth. Panic sizzled through her. She felt the cold anger in his gaze and admitted at last that Jasmine was right; this was a man with something to hide.

"I'm going to let you breathe," he told her curtly. "How is that for starters? But don't scream. Do you understand?"

His thighs were tight about her hips. He kept his weight off her, but she felt the power of his hold. He was in control, so she had to fight another way. She nodded.

He moved his hand away. "Who were you talking to? Who was in here?"

"No one."

"Don't lie to me."

"Why not? You're adept at the art!"

"What?" He sat back slightly and eyed her as he might a particularly difficult puzzle that he was just beginning to unravel. "Ah . . . well, something at last."

"Yes, something!" Carly retorted. It hurt so damn badly. She'd wanted to believe in him more than she had ever wanted anything.

Jasmine was safe, so Carly could meet him with the truth, she realized.

Anger gave her a surge of strength. She freed her hands from the prison of his body and pounded suddenly against his chest. "You liar! Just who the hell are you?"

"What?"

"You aren't Jon Vadim."

Startled, he grabbed her wrists and secured them high over her head, a slow smile starting to play at his lips. She didn't know whether his smile was evil and menacing—or simply amused.

"Who said I wasn't Jon Vadim?"

"You aren't, are you?"

"Who told you?"

"So it is true!" she whispered in dismay.

"Your clandestine visitor has been bearing tales, I see. Damn it, Carly, tell me. Who the hell was here?"

"Admit it! You aren't Jon Vadim."

His eyes narrowed, he released her and rocked back on his haunches. For a man still half dressed in evening clothes, he was very agile, she thought. He could move with great coordination, and at the whisper of a sound. Her heart sank further. He had practiced the art of silent and supple stalking; he was some beast of the night who was at home with crimes in the moonlight.

"What's the matter, Carly? Were you that desperate for a title? Were the name and the money and the castle what really mattered to you?"

"What?" she shrieked.

He placed his hands over her mouth again. "Shut up, will you?"

She slammed his hand away. "You're the crook, and you dare to say something like that to me?"

"It seems true enough."

"You stupid liar! I don't even like this castle, and I hate the horrible basement! Titles don't mean a damn thing to me. I'm an American. But lies and murder, yes—whoever the hell you are!—they do bother me. Tremendously!"

"Murder?" He eyed her warily.

"The real Count Vadim!"

He leaped off the bed as nimbly as a wolf and dragged her along with him. "Come on!" he said roughly. He had her hand.

Panicking, Carly tried desperately to free herself from his hold, but he was striding toward the wall and she couldn't begin to ease the vise of his fingers around her wrist. "Oh, my God! What are you doing?"

He'd seen what she had seen on the balcony, the hard stones far below, and he meant to toss her over. "No!" she cried.

He came to the wall. He touched the light sconce, and a panel silently opened and gave way to a dim corridor beyond.

Carly gasped. She stared at the secret panel, and then at him. He didn't mean to kill her. Not immediately.

He couldn't kill her, she decided. He couldn't have held and touched and loved a woman as he had done with her and intend to snuff out her life.

But he *had* been in her room before; he had come through the panel in the night.

She kicked him. He swore and stared at her in new fury. "What the hell was that for?"

"You've been in here before at night."

"Yes—"

"Oh! As well as being a liar and an impostor, you're also a—"

"I came in to see that you were all right. That you were alive and well, you little fool. Now, let's go." He jerked on her arm, pushing her forward into the passage.

She stopped inside. There was a hint of perfume still on the air here. She knew now where Jasmine had disappeared to. She could see, too, how she had missed the narrow little alley when she'd looked at the structure of the building. It ran the length of the hallway and beyond, but the stones of the castle were so thick as to make the passage undetectable.

He came behind her, and the panel slid shut behind him. The only light in the narrow alley came from shafts near the roof that let in the moon's glow. He shoved Carly in the small of the back, and she started walking.

She stopped suddenly, and he ran into her. She swung around, trembling. "Where are you taking me?"

"You'll see."

"Oh, no I won't. If you're going to kill me, you're going to do it right here and now. I won't help you leave my body in some deserted cave!"

"Oh, for God's sake, I'm not going to kill you! How could you possibly think such a thing? Now, walk!" He pushed her forward again.

Carly felt the adrenaline rushing through her. The floor was rough on her stockinged feet, and she bruised her toe. Crying out softly, she stumbled and grabbed the injured part. Hobbling, she turned on him again. "Who are you?"

"I'll tell you in a few minutes—"

"No! You'll tell me now! What's your name?"

"It is Vadim—"

"Don't lie to me! I know that you're a fake!"

"Fine," he agreed irritably. He caught her arm and took the lead.

Her toe wasn't that bad, she thought, but it would have been nice if he had cared. "My name is Vadim. It just isn't Jon Vadim. I'm Dustin."

"Sure," Carly retorted.

He shrugged. "Have it your way— Watch it!"

He dragged her against him as they passed a sudden hole to one side. Carly gasped, then realized that it was a narrow, winding staircase that probably led to the courtyard. He barely noticed her reaction, but she decided he couldn't mean to kill her. If he had wanted her to die, he could have given her a shove and she would have gone crashing into eternity.

Her heart began pounding too quickly again. She lagged back, gasping for breath. ''Please, whoever you are, just wait—''

''Oh, no, sweetheart. You started this tonight. Let's finish it.''

''No, you started it! You lied!''

That time he stopped. He turned on her, towering over her. Their bodies touched, and his eyes glowed at hers with a searing reproach.

''I told you that others were involved! I told you that nothing about us was a lie. And you just blinked those lovely turquoise eyes and said you loved me. And I believed you. Hell, I didn't want to lie to you. Oh, never mind!''

He swung around again, curling his fingers around hers, and dragged her on down the passageway. He stopped abruptly again and placed his hands against the wall. Carly saw that it was another secret panel.

Light poured in on them. She blinked and saw that they were in his bedroom. No, they were in *Jon Vadim's* bedroom.

And the real Jon Vadim was curled on his bed in his smoking jacket. He held a glass of champagne, and when she and this Vadim first appeared at the far right of his bed, the count didn't notice them. He was in earnest conversation with the dark-haired woman who sat curled up beside him. She, too, held a glass of champagne and was listening to his every word with a tender and forgiving smile.

It was Jasmine.

''Jasmine!'' exclaimed the man at Carly's side. ''I should have known.''

"Oh!" Jasmine spilled her champagne. Nervously she jumped off the foot of the bed, staring at the two visitors. "Dustin. Carly."

"I say there!"

The real Jon Vadim stepped more regally off his bed and rescued the fluted champagne glass from Jasmine. Carly decided at last that "her" Vadim was telling the truth—Jasmine had just called him Dustin.

"Dustin, you've frightened Jasmine. You could have given us some warning," he said reproachfully.

"I'm losing my mind!" Carly muttered.

"I really am sorry—" Jasmine began.

"Well, Jasmine, damn it, this time you should be," Dustin cut in. Hands on hips, he strode into the room. Carly gazed from one man to the other. The two were incredibly alike. Only when they were together could she tell the difference between them. But maybe if she had known that there were two of them, she would have seen more of the subtle differences.

"Twins?" she inquired.

Dustin stopped and stared back at her. "No, not twins. We're cousins. You do see that the real Jon Vadim is alive and well," he said flatly.

"Jasmine," Carly snapped. "What the hell is going on?"

"Carly, please, don't be angry—"

"Don't be angry! You drag me halfway across the world and then disappear and I'm worried sick and then—"

Dustin broke in, angry as well. "And then you decided to drop in on your sister via the secret panel. And you tell her that I'm not Jon, but you neglect to tell her who I really am!" He was shouting by the end of his tirade. His cousin came up to him and grasped his shoulders, shaking his head and murmuring, "Dustin, stop. Someone might hear."

"Dustin, I am sorry," Jasmine said sweetly. "Really. I didn't know who was coming, so I thought I should disappear. I didn't realize I had made Carly think that you were a criminal."

"Please!" Carly implored them. "Will someone please explain this to me?"

Dustin threw up his arms, exasperated.

"Carly, have some champagne," Jasmine suggested, and went to find more glasses. Carly noticed that her sister was completely at home entertaining in Jon Vadim's bedroom. There was something very heavy between Jasmine and Jon Vadim. Carly realized that now. But not between Jasmine and Dustin. In his way, she knew, Dustin had been honest with her. He had asked her to believe. Nonetheless she still felt betrayed, for none of them had trusted her.

"I'll explain," Jon said. He indicated a grouping of chairs before the fireplace. "Sit down, will you, please?"

She must have been staring at them all with a great deal of hostility, for Jasmine added earnestly, "Please, Carly?"

Carly accepted the champagne her sister handed her and sat down. Dustin remained standing stiffly in the middle of the room. Jasmine sat before Carly, and Jon Vadim stood behind Jasmine's chair. "You know that a village girl was killed last year?" he asked Carly.

She frowned. "Yes."

"They blamed Jon," Jasmine broke in, her tone defensive. "Well, there were insinuations, you see. But Jon didn't do it."

"The inspector couldn't find any answers, Carly," Jon continued. "The way that the murder occurred—a full moon, Halloween night and all that—I was afraid of something happening again. It seemed as if I was being used for someone else's lunacy. Do you understand?"

Carly noticed that his eyes were hazel, too, and had the same fascinating golden glow to them as Dustin's. The men were very much alike when they smiled as the real Count Vadim was smiling at her now.

She was about to be charmed a second time, she thought. "Go on. I'm still listening," she said curtly.

"Dustin and I are cousins. We've always been very close. Our fathers were brothers who married sisters, which makes us as close as can be without being siblings, I suppose," he said.

Dustin, still in a foul temper, didn't say a word.

"Anyway," Jon went on, "Dustin used to be in the Queen's special services—"

"British CIA?" Carly interjected.

"Not exactly, but close enough. We didn't even know how much we looked alike until last year. I went to see him in London when he opened his private practice—"

"Private practice?" Carly repeated, staring straight at Dustin.

"Investigations," he said flatly.

"Of course," she murmured.

"I needed help, Carly," Jon Vadim said with dignity.

"So you switched places?"

Jon grinned. "Dustin had to trim his hair and shave his beard, but it worked. Only really close friends and relatives could tell."

"But—"

"Carly," Jasmine said, sighing, "someone attacked me in the barn in the middle of October. I escaped, and I began to wonder if I was imagining things. But I wasn't. Jon knew it, and I knew it. And of course this whole thing has been tense. Jon and I fought, and I decided to leave. I was frightened. I didn't know then about Jon and Dustin changing places."

Carly breathed a little easier. "So you haven't been here all this time?" she asked her sister.

Jasmine shook her head. "I came in last night. I knew something was going on. I was trying to understand what. When I saw that you were here, I was frightened for you."

"But you couldn't stay away from Jon long enough to finish your story to her," Dustin observed dryly.

"I'm sorry! I didn't realize that I was creating a problem."

"Oh, hell, Jasmine!" Dustin protested. "How would I know that you were hiding behind the panels! I was scared to death. I thought the real murderer might be in with your sister."

Jasmine lowered her head. "I'm sorry. I really am."

Carly swallowed her champagne, then looked up at the three of them. "There have been two more murders."

Dustin nodded grimly.

"And do you know who the murderer is?" she asked.

"Someone in the castle," Dustin replied.

"But not Jon," Jasmine said quickly.

"Dustin has a good idea," Jon said.

"Who?"

Dustin shook his head. "I can't say, not until I'm sure. I might cast suspicion on an innocent man, and as Jon can tell you, it isn't pleasant."

"Oh..." Carly murmured uneasily, looking at Jon—the real Jon. She was still in a tangle of emotions over Dustin and didn't want to meet his gaze. "Does the inspector know that there are two of you?"

"No, he doesn't," Jon said. He frowned. "Why?"

"Well, once he knows that there are two 'Jon' Vadims, he will really be suspicious, and no alibi in the world will be believable."

Jasmine groaned miserably.

"There isn't really a problem," Dustin said quickly.

Carly could see now that he didn't want to upset her, however angry he might have been at Jasmine. "Why not?" Carly demanded.

"Because I intend to catch our murderer—by the next full moon." His gaze fell only on Carly. "The murders take place only by the full moon, you know."

Shivering, she bit into her lower lip. By the light of the full moon... And she had to believe that the Vadims were innocent, both Jon, whom Jasmine so clearly adored, and Dustin, who...

She was still in love with him. His name wasn't Jon, and he wasn't the count. But that didn't change anything. She really did hate the castle, her French was atrocious—but Dustin Vadim lived in London.

She lowered her head and realized that she was light-headed with relief and exhausted. And she was still in love; she had really believed in him. Even when she had been confronted by the lie, her instincts had told her that she could hold him, that she could thrill to his kiss and lie down beside him and forget everything else.

It wasn't over. She winced and smoothed a wrinkle in her skirt. She looked up at Dustin at last. "Why didn't you tell me who you were?"

"I couldn't. I didn't know where Jasmine was. She really did go to Paris. I didn't know how to make you understand. You might have thought that we were both demented. You might have gone to the inspector."

She nodded. "Did you steal the letter from my purse?"

He frowned, shaking his head. "No. Jon?"

"No, of course not. I wouldn't have gone into a woman's purse."

Dustin shrugged and grinned. "That's the difference between the nobility in the family and the P.I. I would have gone into your purse if I had thought it necessary. I just didn't."

Carly shivered. "Then someone else was in my room."

"Oh, Carly!" Jasmine said worriedly, glancing with reproach at Jon.

"I told her to go home," Dustin said to Jasmine. "She wouldn't leave without you."

"You should go home," Jasmine told her sister.

"And leave you here?"

"But Carly—"

"If you stay," Dustin interrupted sternly, his gaze still focused on Carly, "you stay with Jasmine."

She started to tremble. She wanted to meet his eyes but couldn't. She knew he meant that she could forgive him, or she could leave.

She could sleep with him here. . . .

Or he would send her home alone. And she would take the chance that she would never see him again. Never feel the sweet tempest of his touch again or know the golden-glowing fire of his eyes. "I—I can't leave now," she said.

"But Carly—" Jasmine began.

Carly realized her sister hadn't understood Dustin's words.

"It's all right, Jasmine," Dustin said. He came over to Carly and reached for her hand. "I'll be with her. Carly, come on. Let's let these two..." He paused, then shrugged. "Let's let them get to bed." He didn't wait for her assent. He took her hand and pulled her to her feet. "Good night," he said to Jasmine and Jon.

The two were silent and Carly couldn't believe that she was silent, too, as Dustin propelled her back through the secret door. She remembered that she had wanted to wring her sister's neck. Once they were all out of this alive, she was going to do just that.

Chapter 10

Carly remained silent as they returned to her room through the narrow secret passageway. Dustin kept his hand on hers, thinking it was a show of bravado on her part. He wondered when she would speak and whether she would revile him, hate him.

He hadn't meant to fall in love with her.

He hadn't even meant to be here.

But Jon had been in trouble, and although the entire plan had seemed incredible at first, it had worked. Or it had been working. At least there was still a good possibility that he would be able to prove Jon's innocence. There was nothing wrong with Jon's determination or courage, but he didn't have Dustin's connections with other law-enforcement agencies and he hadn't spent the years as Dustin had, learning to listen for the smallest detail, to watch and wait and move in silence.

Carly's hand felt cold in his.

Well, at least she had not refused him. She was here, at his side. Perhaps the awkward quiet between them was growing combustible. Perhaps she had every right to be mad. Well, all right, furious. He just hadn't had any choice. He was too close to the truth.

He struck the wall with his hand and the panel to her room opened. She walked on in ahead of him, her stockinged tread a whisper.

He followed her and stood waiting. He watched her as she paced to and fro. It was a mistake, for it made his mouth grow dry, and all he could think of was that things couldn't have happened any other way. From the moment he had stumbled upon her he had been enchanted. Her turquoise eyes had been a dangerous sea that had beckoned him like an unwary sailor. He could still see the way her hair had tumbled over her shoulders in the moonlight. She had seemed a creature born of the moonlight, born of the mists and even of the dangers in the secretive forest, a storm, but sweet beyond belief.

No, he thought ruefully, he hadn't meant to fall in love. He had wanted her to go home; he had warned her to go home. And now he was terrified that she would do so. He had never before worried about the future with a woman, and now he knew that he *had* been waiting; before, everything had been child's play compared to this emotion. It wasn't the color of her eyes, though that was extraordinary. It wasn't the gold in her hair that glowed softly by moonlight and brilliantly beneath the sun. Nor was it the delicate perfection of her face or the slim, supple elegance of her form. It was the way she smiled at him shyly when she trusted him, and opened up about past wounds. It was in the way that she laughed and wound her arms around him so openly. It was in her eyes when humor filled them, and passion and tenderness.

She quit pacing and spun on him at last. "You could have told me!"

He shook his head. "No. I couldn't."

"You asked me to trust you. But you didn't trust *me* enough."

"I trusted you. Carly, I told you. I wasn't in it alone. And it's a very dangerous game. They still hang convicted murderers here. I'm playing with Jon's life."

She lowered her head, and he couldn't see her eyes or, therefore, read her heart.

"I'm playing with my own life, too, I suppose," he added. "Once the inspector realizes that I'm here . . ."

"You know the inspector?"

He started to smile.

"As yourself, I mean." She sighed, exasperated. "Does the inspector know Dustin Vadim?"

He nodded. He wasn't accustomed to begging, and he wasn't going to beg her to forgive him.

He was ready to come damned close to it, though.

"I told you," he said huskily, "Jon and I are close. I used to come here all the time when I was young."

"You don't think that the inspector suspects something?" Carly said.

Dustin shook his head. "Not even Jon and I realized how much we resemble each other until he came to London last year. I knew that I was coming to help in some capacity. When we were kids, I was kind of the runt. I think I'm still a quarter of an inch shorter. And I always wore my hair longer. I'd had a beard and a mustache until I shaved it off the night we worked out this scheme."

Carly nodded, wandering over to the bed.

The next thing Dustin knew he had a pillow in his face. He staggered back—she could throw hard. "Carly—"

"You son of a—! I don't even remember all the things that I said to him, when I thought I was talking to you."

"You never said anything—"

"How do you know? I thought you were crazy at times. You could have very easily been a homicidal lunatic, because you had no memory whatsoever."

"Carly—"

"Damn you! Damn the two of you!"

He stiffened. She stood next to the bed and stared at him hard, a glaze of tears adding color to the depths of her eyes. He wanted to rush over and hold her, but knew he couldn't. She hadn't forgiven him, and she didn't want him touching her.

He picked up the pillow awkwardly. "I'll just take this over by the doorway. I'd leave you alone, except that I'm afraid to. I don't want you in any danger."

She watched him walk across the room, position himself on the floor and pound the pillow. She stared for several seconds.

"I have to stay here," he repeated. "Carly, I know you hate me right now, but I'm afraid to leave you."

She shook her head. "What the hell are you doing?"

"I'm going to sleep here!"

Dustin watched as she slowly approached him. She was in her stocking feet, but she wore the black dress beautifully, and though her hair was mussed and wild, he thought that she had never appeared more elegant or sexier. She paused and knelt down by him. There still seemed to be a glaze about her eyes, but she was smiling, too.

"You're going to sleep on the floor. Why?" she said.

"Because I can't leave—"

"Yes, yes, you told me that. I believe you. I don't want you to leave."

"Then—"

"It's just that—why the floor? There's a perfectly good bed just a few feet away."

He paused, all his senses taking flight. His heart jumped into his throat, and a swift, rigid ache jutted into his loins. He wanted to reach out and touch her; he was afraid he would drag her down. He stared up at her instead, afraid to move.

"Is that some kind of an invitation?" he asked.

"I suppose it is."

He didn't dare move. She leaned forward and stroked his cheek. "Yes. I suppose it is," she said once again.

"But I thought . . ."

"What?"

"I thought you were mad."

"I am." A mischievous smile touched her lips, and she curled up beside him as sinuously graceful as a cat. "Mad, angry, irate, furious, et cetera. But . . ."

"But?" he asked, not daring to breathe.

"But I think I love you, anyway."

"You think?"

"I could use some persuasion at the moment."

He touched her. He cupped her skull and held her fast and kissed her, drowning in the kiss. She had opened the door; he stepped through with a flourish. They rolled on the floor, and he drank in the heady taste of her. His hands ravaged her legs, stroking, tearing at her hose. The silk of her gown slid over his flesh, smooth and cool, while the silk of her skin seared and warmed and inflamed him.

He got to his knees, pulling her with him. She smiled languidly.

"There is a perfectly good bed," he said.

"Mmm," she agreed.

He strode to the bed and set her upon it. She slipped her fingers to the buttons of his shirt to undo them. "It's a pity," she said on a sigh.

"A pity?"

She feathered her fingertips over his flesh, just here, just there, a merciless tease. "Yes. I'm just as furious with Jasmine and Jon."

"Uh-huh?..."

She slid the edges of her nails beneath the waistband of his trousers and eased them around. "They behaved horribly, too."

"They did. Horribly." He reached behind her, ruffling her hair, found the zipper to her gown and pulled it down with a rasp. He heard the same sound as she found his fly. It was the most erotic sound he had ever heard.

"But *they* have the champagne," Carly said.

"Do you want some champagne?" he asked.

"Umm..." she murmured, mulling it over. Her fingers feathered over and around him.

He groaned deep in his throat and drew her close. "Carly?"

"Yes?"

"The hell with the champagne." He cast their clothing aside and swept her fiercely beneath him.

Outside, somewhere on a distant mountain, a great silver wolf howled at the half moon, and the night passed swiftly.

The two weeks that followed were curiously tender and painfully tense for Dustin and Carly. Although they could easily have convinced the inspector that Jasmine was not a corpse, Jon decided that she should remain in hiding, so Carly saw her sister by slipping through the secret passageway to his room.

Tanya grew moody and bored and complained that she wanted to go home—or to the south of France or the Costa del Sol or Monte Carlo, or anywhere that was away. Tanya was petulant and spoiled, but Carly still felt sorry for her. Tanya had been good to her. But none of them was going anywhere—the inspector had taken their passports and they were obliged to remain within the boundaries of the duchy.

Dustin arranged a riding party and picnic. They saw a film at the one movie theater in the village. They dined in elegance each night, and each night Dustin slipped up to her room.

Night was the magic time for them. Carly knew that by day he was listening and watching and waiting, even if she didn't know what he listened or watched or waited for. The closer she grew to the others, the less she could believe that any of them could be evil.

She thought that Tanya must be growing bored even with her lover, for Carly no longer heard her meet anyone in the hall. But then, maybe Carly herself was involved enough not to see or hear anything else. She hadn't paid the least bit of attention to any major news in the world at large, so perhaps it was natural that she wouldn't notice what went on outside her room.

The secret passageways led all over the castle, Carly discovered, so it was easy for Jon to reach the library and put in a day's work—since Dustin really knew very little about running the estate. One morning when Dustin had to go into the village—to send a telegram, he told her vaguely—Carly went down to the library and had breakfast with Jasmine and Jon.

She was amazed now that she had ever thought that the two men were exactly alike. The more she knew them, the more the differences became apparent. But then, she was in love with only one of them. She knew the little things that a lover discovered, a freckle just beneath the hairline, a tiny scar here, a mole there. And she knew the different inflections in their voices and even the differences in the way they moved.

Dustin had a tendency to swagger, she decided with amusement. Then she wondered whether she would ever tell him so.

No . . . she'd let him swagger a little, she decided.

"You're smiling," Jasmine complained.

Carly realized that her sister had been growing very tense.

"Sweetheart, you could have stayed in Paris," Jon reminded her.

Jasmine sat back in her chair, then shivered. "It's just that this goes on and on! If only it would end!"

Jon walked around behind her and placed his hands on her shoulders. "It will end." He hesitated. "The moon will be full tonight."

Now it was Carly's turn to shiver. She suddenly felt as if she were suffocating. She mumbled some excuse to the two of them and ran out of the room.

In the hallway, she nearly collided with Geoffrey. "Hi, stranger," he said, his dark eyes warm.

"Oh, Geoffrey." She flushed, hoping he didn't want to go into the library. She slipped her arm through his and started walking toward the terrace. "I've been doing sketches for the play."

"You have?" He seemed surprised.

"You do still want me," she said.

"Of course, of course. I just didn't know—well, it's none of my business, of course, but I didn't know if you would be coming back to the States or not."

Carly lowered her head as a little river of uncertainty flowed through her. What would her future be? Her little apartment, on the fourth floor of an old brownstone, seemed so far away. She had worried about being in love with a count. Rushing off to become a countess was something far more likely for Jasmine to do than for her. Dustin wasn't the count, so she needn't go into trauma worrying about that, but still . . .

He was English. He worked in London. He had never said anything about the future. She believed that what they had was solid and real, but she had no idea whether or not he meant it to be forever.

"Well," she said, "I'm certainly still quite anxious to work on the show." She offered him a dazzling smile. "To think, Geoffrey, I feel that I know you so very well. And I was in such great awe of you before I came here. A Broadway producer and director. I'm still in awe."

He laughed, and she was reminded of the way he had looked on the night they had first met, all wrapped up in his mummy rags. He was handsome and very warm, and she thought, giving Geoffrey an affectionate smile, that if she hadn't been so swept away by storm, she might have taken a much slower route. She liked Geoffrey very much. Maybe not forever, but as a good friend.

"Run up and get the sketches," he suggested. "I'd love to see them. We can meet in the library."

"No!" Carly realized how horribly guilty she sounded. "No—I'd much rather be on the terrace. Wouldn't you?"

"Well, it's a little cold—"

"But the sun is out. Would you mind terribly?"

"No, of course not. I'll be waiting."

When she came back down with her sketches, he was seated at the dining table on the terrace. Marie had brought out some hot chocolate.

"Spiked," Geoffrey assured her.

It was spiked, with brandy, and it was delicious.

The afternoon passed easily. She and Geoffrey went over the sketches, and he pointed out where she might have a few problems with some of the stage business he had planned. He grew excited, describing the production so clearly that she could see it in her mind's eye. She modified her work as he talked, and when evening came around, she was very excited and had done a tremendous amount of work.

"I can't wait to look for fabrics...." she said, erasing to adjust a train for an evening gown.

"Alexi! Hello there!" Geoffrey said.

Carly glanced up. Alexi, in a red sweater and jeans, was coming from the hallway. He smiled at her.

"Hello. May I join you?"

"Of course," Carly said.

He sat down and planted his feet on another chair and looked at them glumly. "The inspector has men following me," he said.

"Oh, surely he wouldn't be doing such a thing!" Carly protested, then she wondered why she had. After all, she was the only one in the group who wasn't a suspect, and that was simply because she hadn't been there last Halloween.

Had Dustin been there? she wondered.

"I'm willing to bet that he also has men eyeing Jon," Alexi said. "Somewhere around here."

"Why do you say that?" Geoffrey asked.

"Because the moon will be full, and that's when the murderer strikes." Alexi said the words with certainty.

A shiver ran down Carly's spine. She glanced at Alexi's hands, where they rested on the table. They were large, powerful hands, she thought. He was a deceptive-looking man. He was young and striking and appeared to be lean and wiry. But he wasn't really slim at all. He was rock solid and strong.

Her heart began to beat a little too swiftly. Dustin suspected him, she thought. Dustin refused to say, but she suddenly felt that she knew he suspected Alexi. So did the inspector. He had men following Alexi.

But then, according to Alexi, men were watching Jon Vadim. Or Dustin Vadim.

And the moon was going to be full....

"Where is Jon?" Alexi asked.

"He's gone into the village," Carly said.

"Will he be back soon?"

"I don't know," she told him. He probably should have been back hours ago, she reflected. How long did it take to send a telegram?

"Why?" Geoffrey asked.

"Oh...I've had some trouble with some of the masonry in my hallway. Jon had work done just last year. He sent to France for a specialist, and I wanted to get Jon's opinion and the name of the firm that did the work." Alexi smiled vaguely. "It isn't really that important. I wanted company more than anything, I suppose."

Geoffrey and Carly both nodded sympathetically. "Perhaps," Geoffrey murmured, "we should all make sure that we stay together tonight."

"All night?" Alexi laughed.

"Why not? We'll have a slumber party in the formal dining room," Geoffrey said.

"Will that do any good?" Carly asked. The other two looked at her, and she flushed. "I suppose that technically the moon is only really a full moon one night. But it gives the appearance of being a full moon for several nights."

They both stared at her. She felt acutely uneasy.

Alexi turned away. "I'm sure they're watching this place. What with the Vadim history..." He shrugged.

"The history?"

"Yes, of course, insanity. And maybe a legend doesn't even have to be true. Maybe a man only has to believe it to go over the brink. The wolves have always prowled these forests, and strike out of the mist. The people in the village believe. They've kept those crosses on their doors for centuries. He doesn't have to be a wolf; he needs only to *think* he's a wolf. The moon makes us all restless." Alexi leaned forward. Even as he'd spoken, it seemed that darkness began to fall and the inevitable low mist began to sweep in enchanting swirls along the ground beyond the terrace.

A sudden crashing sound behind her sent Carly spinning around. Tanya was there. She stared past them. And looked as if she had seen a ghost. She had dropped a glass of wine.

"Tanya? What is it?" Carly asked.

She shook her head. "Sorry. I'm seeing things in the mist, I suppose." She stooped to pick up the glass. Marie, who had apparently heard the crash, came running in. Telling Tanya and Carly that they must not bother, she quickly swept up the mess.

"You would like more wine, *mam'selle*?" Marie asked.

Tanya sank into a chair near Carly. "Yes, darling, I would. Thank you so much." She stared across the table at Alexi.

Carly didn't know exactly what it was about that look, but she was suddenly certain that the man Tanya had been meeting at night was Alexi. And perhaps she had been sneaking him in because supposedly he hadn't been at the castle all those nights—although he was a frequent visitor and he was always welcome to stay, he did have his own home, and he did go to it.

Or so it had seemed.

He had stayed away more than usual lately, Carly noted.

"Have you come for—dinner?" Tanya asked him blandly. She was in denim, but she managed to make denim look ultrachic, even elegant, Carly observed.

"I'm not dressed," Alexi murmured, then shrugged. "I'm sure Jon will have something. Yes, I will stay." He looked back at Carly. "The full moon, you know."

The way he said it gave her chills. She stood, collecting her drawings. "I think I'll...shower," she said lamely.

"Sounds good to me," Geoffrey said, standing, too. Then he laughed. "I didn't mean that I was following you to your shower," he assured Carly with a smile. "I mean, I'm going to go shower. By myself."

Carly laughed, waved uneasily to the three of them and headed for the stairway. She paused and glanced back. Geoffrey had already left. Two dark heads were bowed there together, Tanya's and Alexi's.

Carly wanted to scream. She wanted to warn Tanya. Yet what could she say? What proof did she have?

Then even as she watched them the two parted. Alexi started toward the main house, and Tanya wandered toward the stairway.

Quickly, so that she wouldn't be caught spying, Carly hurried through the rest of the terrace and headed upstairs.

The castle seemed dark that evening—the lights hadn't been turned on yet. There were shadows everywhere, it seemed. And it seemed as if the mist from outside had penetrated the walls to rise on the stairs. She knew it wasn't real. And that she wasn't alone, not at all. Tanya was right behind her.

Carly still felt as if demons were breathing down her neck. She rushed into her room and closed the door. Once she'd set down her drawings, she drew up her knees as she sat thoughtfully at the foot of the bed.

It had to be Alexi. She would confront Dustin with her belief that night.

But something nagged at her, and she didn't know what.

Then she realized what it was.

Tanya. Tanya had dropped her glass because she had seen something. They had all been together then, she and Geoffrey and Alexi and Tanya. Jon and Jasmine and Dustin had been missing.

So what? she charged herself. Tanya might have seen anything. A movement in that eternal mist.

Carly rose. She went to the balcony doors and opened them. The mist was rising. It didn't entirely obscure her view; it just cast a curious opaque veil over the world. She could still see the stables across the courtyard. And she could see the cars drawn up in front. The Lamborghini was there, as well as the Volvo and Alexi's Peugeot.

She narrowed her eyes. She thought she could see the Mercedes—the car that Dustin had taken that morning—parked beside the stables. She wondered why he would park there, then shrugged. Maybe it didn't matter.

She started to turn away when a sudden movement caught her attention. A woman was running from the house to the stables. Carly stared harder.

It was Jasmine.

Her sister—who was supposedly in hiding, who was supposedly not here—was running outdoors. Jasmine had been restless, Carly knew. Very restless. Jasmine considered the world to be her oyster, and even if she did really love Count Vadim, she could not bear being penned in for long.

"But you're in danger here, you silly goose!" Carly whispered.

Jasmine disappeared through the stable door. Carly hesitated just a moment, then, deciding to go after her sister, she left her room and raced down the stairway. She came out on the terrace and ran down the steps to the courtyard, breathing heavily.

It had grown dark quickly. It was still twilight, but the gray swirl of the coming night had already descended.

Carly looked up. The moon was shining, glowing down upon the courtyard already. The full moon.

"Jasmine...damn you!" Carly muttered nervously.

She reached the stables and tried the door. It wouldn't give. She jiggled the handle. Nothing happened.

"Jasmine!" she whispered. "Jasmine!" Her voice grew louder, and still there was no answer.

Then she heard her sister scream.

The sound was a long and shrill and filled with terror. It came once then again and again.

"Jasmine!"

Carly threw her entire weight against the door. She heard a shuddering and splintering of old wood, and then the door caved in.

She had put so much effort into the blow that the force sent her flying to the ground. She skinned her palms, though she barely noticed.

It was dark inside the barn. The moon's glow only touched the doorway. The lights should have been on, she knew. One of the horses whinnied. Another shuffled. Another gave a nervous snort.

"Jasmine!" Carly screamed.

"Carly!"

Suddenly Jasmine came hurtling toward her. Carly had just begun to rise, but her sister's weight sent her flying. There was a flurry of motion. Dirt choked her throat, and Jasmine's form completely blinded her.

"You're all right!" Carly cried, hugging her sister. Jasmine was shaking, horribly, terribly. Carly realized that she herself was shaking, too. Jasmine began to speak disjointedly.

"I—I had to get out. Just for a few seconds. I thought I could slip in here and see the horses. Oh, it was like last time, before I ran. When I wrote you. I was so scared. I was terrified. Oh, Carly, he grabbed me. He had a knife. He had it up to my throat. Until someone ripped him from me. Until you came. If you hadn't come when you did . . ."

"We've got to get out of here!" Carly murmured.

Jasmine pulled away and studied her sister with wide eyes. "Oh, Carly—" She broke off. There were footsteps by the doorway.

He was silhouetted there in the moonlight. Though she couldn't see his features, Carly knew that it was Dustin.

He rushed in and fell to his knees beside the two of them. He lifted Jasmine's chin. "Are you all right?"

She nodded. "But who—"

"I don't know," he said.

"It was you. It was you in here," Carly said, recalling that it had been his car she'd seen. And she also recalled the flurry of movement that had made Tanya drop her glass.

He glanced at her impatiently. In the darkness his gaze was golden and luminescent, like the wolf's. "Yes, I was here. And I almost had him. But he had Jasmine."

Carly sank back, swallowing. I love this man! she reminded herself. But he had been there, and someone had attacked her sister. Had he really saved Jasmine, or had he been the one attacking her?

"Come on. Let's get out of here," Dustin urged them, helping her to her feet. The three started walking back toward the castle. Figures appeared in the mist. As they came closer, Carly saw that it was Geoffrey and Alexi.

"Cat's out of the bag now," Dustin murmured.

"What happened?" Geoffrey demanded, rushing forward. "I heard the screaming."

"Jasmine!" Alexi cried out.

He sounded concerned, very innocent. Carly didn't know what to think. "Someone attacked Jasmine in the barn," she explained.

"Why, how preposterous!" Geoffrey exclaimed. "Jasmine isn't even supposed to be here." He paused.

"What are you doing here, my dear? You were in Paris—weren't you?"

Jasmine nodded. She nervously fingered her throat and leaned forward to kiss his cheek. "Hello, Geoffrey. I've, er, just arrived."

"And to such a thing!" Alexi murmured. He seemed to be breathing too hard, Carly decided.

But then again, so was Dustin.

Feeling as if her skin crawled, she looked at the lot of them. Any one of them could have attacked her sister, run away and reappeared. Any one of them.

Dustin had been in the barn.

"Let's bring her inside," he said.

Jasmine cast him a grateful glance and started to say his name. He frowned and she quickly corrected herself. "Jon, how sweet. I'd love a brandy."

"Of course. And we have to report this to the inspector."

"Oh, for heaven's sake!" Alexi complained. "He'll make us all insane again. And besides, he should know. He has men around somewhere, I believe."

The inspector did have men around. The two who had been assigned to Alexi came running into the courtyard then. Carly decided they must have been playing cards or something, for they hadn't even heard Jasmine screaming.

The inspector was called, and he did put them all through a million questions again. Carly felt guilty, as if she were lying, though really she wasn't. But she knew that the man he was calling "Count" was Dustin Vadim and that there were two Vadims. There was always an extra Vadim....

A man who didn't need an alibi, since no one except Carly and Jasmine knew about the deception.

There was no formal dinner that evening. Marie brought roast beef sandwiches and spicy pasta salads while the inspector continued to interrogate them.

Alexi had been right about one thing. It was the same vein of questioning, over and over. The inspector threatened, cajoled, and in the end was frustrated.

Jasmine went upstairs with Carly when it was time for bed, and Carly was glad.

Jasmine was still fingering her throat nervously as she said, "I was so frightened. It was really almost over for us this evening. Jon heard the commotion, of course, and almost came out. He was so afraid for me."

Was he? Carly wondered. Where *had* Jon Vadim been? Were she and Jasmine both mesmerized?

Jasmine kissed her suddenly. "I've got to go to him."

"Jasmine! No. Tonight you should stay with me—"

"No, no, I can't. He's been worried sick. I'll see you first thing in the morning. I have to be with him, too. I have to be his alibi." She slipped through the paneling.

Carly stared after her. His alibi? Or his victim? she wondered.

And she realized that she was thinking the same thing herself.

She bathed and dressed in her flannel gown. Dustin hadn't come to her, and she shivered, not knowing whether it was from anticipation or fear.

He had been in the stables. He had been there....

She opened the door to the balcony. The moon was up high now. So very full. Its light was cast down on the courtyard, and she was certain that she was bathed in its glow, too.

"Carly..."

Her breath caught, and she spun around. Dustin walked across to her and buried his face in her throat. "You're so beautiful here, so very, very beautiful."

He held her shoulders and drew her to him to kiss her lips and the furiously pounding pulse at her throat. He untied the ribbon at her neck, the flannel nightgown fell to her feet and she was naked in the moonlight.

He lowered his head and took her breast into his mouth. His tongue laved her nipple, which hardened into an erotic peak. The warmth feathered and spread into her loins, and she did not feel the chill of the night; she knew only the radiant heat of his mouth upon her. His lips traveled over her, and he fell to his knees. He caressed and explored her form, pressing her forward. The taunting, intimate warmth of his tongue seared into her and she cried out, throwing back her head. She was heedless of the moon, of the night, aware only of the man who stroked her into endless pleasure.

She collapsed on him, and he carried her in. They made love with the doors open and the moonlight falling upon them.

A chill grew in the room. Dustin rose, naked and sleek, closed the doors, and they made love again.

Carly must have drifted off. She awoke, vaguely aware that he was moving. "What is it?" she asked him.

"Thirsty," he muttered, then kissed her. "Tonight I think I'll get that champagne."

He crawled out of bed. Carly sank farther beneath the covers. She could hear wolves howling. There were many of them tonight, it seemed. The sound was loud and haunting, and she could well imagine them out there, bathed in the light of the moon.

"Be right back," Dustin promised.

Exhausted, Carly murmured something, then closed her eyes and slept.

When she awoke she was disoriented. The night was almost over, and the room was filling with dawn's rosy light.

Some sound alerted her, and she sat up, grasping the covers to her.

Dustin was at the foot of the bed, smiling ruefully, holding a bottle and two champagne glasses. She smiled back lazily and relaxed. "I think we should have started earlier. It's almost morning."

"So it is," Dustin agreed. He threw off his robe and kicked off his brown leather slippers. Carly frowned slightly. There was mud on them.

"Here!" Naked, he crawled back in beside her. He pressed a glass of champagne into her hands and poured his own. He clinked glasses with her, and she sipped. It didn't taste half bad in the morning, she thought. He leaned over and kissed her, and he tasted of champagne. She smiled as the champagne bubbled through her, feather light, dry, pleasant. She was only half awake. She felt comfortable and secure.

She couldn't believe that she had ever let herself worry or wonder about Dustin. She loved him.

She swallowed the rest of the champagne and realized that he was studying her with his wolf's gaze, eyes slightly narrowed, features tense. She knew what was coming when he plucked the glass from her fingers, and met his kiss eagerly, anticipating its lush heat.

She could be exhausted or furious or even barely awake, but all he needed to do was touch her and she came alive. He held her body and came down upon her and filled her with passion, raw and exciting. And when it was over, she didn't realize that the room was filled with daylight; she closed her eyes and fell asleep once more.

She didn't wake until much later. Someone was shaking her.

She blinked, then pulled the covers up high about her.

Jasmine was sitting at the foot of her bed.

"Oh, it's awful!" Jasmine moaned worriedly. "Carly, you have to wake up. You have to get dressed and come down. He's waiting."

"Who's waiting?" Carly asked cautiously. "And what is awful?"

Jasmine got off the bed so that Carly could rise. "The inspector is waiting. And it's awful because— Oh, Carly! Tanya was murdered last night."

Tanya!

Ice entered her heart and curled around it. Tanya couldn't be dead. Not spoiled, petulant Tanya, who could also be so kind. No, she couldn't be dead....

"The coroner knows she was killed sometime during the middle of the night. Oh, Carly! See why I had to go to Jon? I know he is innocent. I was with him all night. And Dustin! See, Carly? You were together all night, so you know!"

The ice clenched her heart like a fist. No, she didn't know that. She didn't know that at all. Dustin had left her in the middle of the night.

In the middle of the night, when the wolves had howled and the moon had been full.

Chapter 11

Once again they were all seated around the library.

Well, not all of them, for poor Tanya was dead and the real Jon Vadim was—to Carly—conspicuously missing.

It was pathetic. Poor Tanya had been found like the victims before her. So far the police were convinced that she'd been killed where she'd been found, in the Carpathian caves deep in the forest.

On Vadim property.

Carly watched Dustin where he sat behind the desk, impressive in a muted tweed plaid, a duster tossed carelessly around his shoulders as if he planned to go out or had been called in from the cold.

Carly felt ill. She wished she hadn't had to confront him here first, in front of the inspector. She'd wanted to scream at him, wanted to pound against his chest.

Every time she looked at him she accused him with her eyes. Where were you last night? Did you disappear in time to commit murder and then return? How could you? Oh, God, poor Tanya!...

And yesterday, when Jasmine had been attacked, he had been in the stables. He had been there, and he had disappeared last night. No, she had to believe in him. As blindly, as loyally as Jasmine believed in the real Jon.

But the real Jon had probably lain with her all night. She had not awakened with dawn's first light to see that he had returned to her, after he'd left by the light of the moon.

The full moon.

Nervous, she jumped to her feet, heedless of what the inspector was saying. It was probably the same old thing. Where were you? What did you do? What happened? They had all gone to bed! It was the simplest damn answer in the world, yet sometime after they had all retired for the night, Tanya had come out of her room again and someone had gone with her for a walk in the woods.

"I don't understand this!" Carly cried. All eyes turned to her. The inspector, so rudely interrupted, cleared his throat. Carly ignored him. "People keep dying, and nothing is done! Don't you have forensic experts? Can't you compare hair or blood samples, or fibers, or—"

"We do try, Madame Kiernan. We do try," the inspector interrupted her coldly. He gave her an acid smile. "In fact, Madame, we have a young American on our staff, so I'm sure that we are as up-to-date as we can be. But sometimes there are no hairs and no fibers. Sometimes the victims die as quickly as if a wolf had leaped out of the forest and stolen their breath away. Then there are the elements, *madame*. Evidence is lost

in the mist that plagues us by twilight and at dawn.
Perhaps you have some suggestion."

Dustin made an aggravated sound, as if he were about
to protest the inspector's tone. But Carly didn't need to
be defended. She set her hands firmly on her hips.
"*Oui, monsieur*, I do. Protection. Everyone believed
something would happen last night, and it did."

Geoffrey let out a pained sound. "You should have
had your eye on the castle!" Carly told the inspector.

Now the inspector seemed pained. "We were watching the castle," he admitted.

"Then?"

He shrugged. "I do not know." He gazed Dustin's
way. "But it seems that the count had an alibi for his
time."

"Yes, he was with me," Jasmine said. Carly colored
and turned toward Jasmine, for the same words had
almost left her own mouth. Jasmine instantly realized
her mistake, but it was too late; the inspector was already sniffing as if he smelled something sour—a lie.

"Well, we were all together for quite some time,"
Jasmine said defensively.

Alexi snorted. "I'd like to hear this."

Carly didn't know whether he had been there all night
or had been summoned by the inspector. She turned to
face him. "Alexi, you should know something about
Tanya's nightly habits."

"What?" His handsome young face flooded with
color. He crossed and uncrossed his legs.

"You were visiting her at night."

"What's this?" the inspector demanded.

"Carly." Dustin cleared his throat and rose. "Carly,
be careful. You're making wild accusations."

No, she wasn't. If Dustin wasn't guilty, then Alexi was. And she desperately wanted Alexi to be guilty. "You were meeting Tanya in her room at night."

All eyes were on Alexi. He shook his head fervently. "I was having an affair with her! I would never hurt her. I was mad about Tanya. I'm the only one here who is really injured by her death. I cared for her!"

"She was wild and impetuous and often cruel," the inspector said. "Maybe she scorned you. Maybe you killed her for that reason."

"Don't be ridiculous! Jon is the one who—" He broke off.

Carly saw that Dustin tensed and rose to come around his desk.

"Go on, Alexi. I'm waiting. Jon what? I'd like to hear the rest."

Alexi shook his head and hung it down. "Nothing. *Rien*. There is nothing at all." He turned back to his seat, dejected. Heavy silence fell on the room.

And then the inspector turned slowly to Dustin. "Count, I will have to ask you to come with me."

Carly gasped. Jasmine leaped to her feet. Dustin stiffened, and it took Geoffrey, quiet until now, to offer a protest. "I say there, old boy, you can't do that. You have no proof whatsoever against Count Vadim, and you can't go dragging him off like that on idle suspicion."

"Count?" the inspector said, ignoring Geoffrey. "You will come with me to the station, please. I have a few more questions."

Dustin hesitated. "Of course."

The inspector turned to the others. "I may want to speak to you all again, later. Please—"

"*Mais oui*, don't leave the village," Alexi said bitterly.

"*Non, monsieur,*" the inspector replied dryly. "Do not leave the castle. *Vous comprenez?*"

No one replied. The inspector rose and Dustin followed, stopping before Carly.

"Count Vadim?" the inspector said again.

Dustin's eyes were on her, golden, glowing. They were the eyes of the wolf, challenging her, searing into her with their glowing fire.

"*Un moment, s'il vous plaît,*" he said quietly. He turned around, facing the inspector. "I want a minute alone. If you will all excuse me?"

Carly was aware of a startled silence, then realized that they were all leaving. She was left alone with Dustin and with the sudden distance that had arisen between them. A distance created by the night, when the man she loved had disappeared with the silence and grace of the silver wolf.

She had slept with him night after night, she reminded herself. She had found rapture in his arms, tenderness and love and laughter. She had found passion as swift and sure as spreading brushfire, and she had found a man who was sensitive to her every mood.

Now she faced him with fear and suspicion creating an unbridgeable distance between them.

She heard the door close softly. They were alone.

"Where did you go?" she demanded, her eyes on his. She kept her voice low. "Last night, you were gone so long. And there was mud on your slippers. Where did you go?"

He smiled—or, rather, his lip curled—and his eyes grew cold. "I went for champagne."

"And muddied your slippers?"

He didn't answer her. He kept his eyes on her, and shrugged. "You believe that I did it. That I sneaked out of the house, found Tanya and murdered her."

She shook her head in denial. "I—I don't know what I believe."

"But you didn't say anything to the inspector."

Carly hesitated. She wanted to touch him. She wanted to reach out and fall into his arms, and then she wanted him to give her a foolproof and marvelous explanation of where he had been.

And why there was mud on his slippers.

"Dustin—"

"I came down for champagne, Carly. I stepped outside for a minute. That's all."

He didn't touch her, and he had no valid explanation. She waited. He set his jaw and said no more.

There was a rapping at the door. "Count Vadim!" the inspector called. "Time is relevant. Please come along."

Then Dustin did touch her. He seized her and drew her against him. "Take care! For the love of God, take care today. Be with someone you trust. Stay near Jasmine. Make sure that you are seen. Do you understand me?"

He shook her, and she nodded, telling herself he couldn't be so vehement and also be guilty of the crimes.

He kissed her, suddenly, savagely. He released her just as the door opened and the inspector stuck his head in. "Count?"

Dustin stepped back. Carly put her hand to her mouth. Dustin turned, and as she watched his broad-shouldered back disappear, she thought with a sick feeling that the inspector had condemned him—he was, in that man's eyes at least, guilty beyond a doubt.

Alone in the library, Carly was forced to make an admission to herself. According to her book, he should be guilty. He'd been gone last night. He'd had the time.

And he had been in the stables when Jasmine had screamed. . . .

She swallowed, then decided that she could clear him if she could just get someone to tell her that Dustin hadn't been there last Halloween, when the first murder had taken place.

She stepped out of the library. The hallway was empty.

"Carly!" It was Alexi calling to her.

She turned around, then shook her head and walked away, her heart pounding. She didn't want to talk to him. He was the one who'd always been talking about werewolves and lunacy and madness. It had to be him, because it could not be Dustin.

"Carly!"

He was following her. Panic seized her. She spun around. "No, Alexi! Leave me alone!"

She turned and fled. As fast as she could, she headed for the stairs and raced up them. When she reached the landing, she ran straight into Geoffrey.

"Geoffrey!" she said.

He caught her and steadied her, smiling. "Sorry. I was just on the phone. Calling home. A bit of a problem, you know."

She nodded.

"Don't be upset," he told her. "They can't hold Jon long."

"What?" she murmured vaguely. His use of the name Jon startled her, for she knew that it was Dustin and not Jon Vadim who had just left with the inspector.

"I said don't worry—they have no proof. They can't hold Jon without proof of some kind."

She looked at Geoffrey and smiled. She had to know the truth about the previous year. "Geoffrey, can I ask you a question?"

"Shoot. Oh, bad choice of a word. Well, not that anyone has been shot, but—"

"Geoffrey, please, it doesn't matter. What I wanted to know about was last year. Last Halloween. Who was here?"

"For last year's party? Oh, well, lots of people. The McCorkindales, Lord and Lady Ashberry, the duke himself, and the duchess, of course, and then there was the American toilet paper manufacturer and—"

"No, no, I'm sorry. I don't mean the casual guests. I mean, who was here, like this year? The closer friends. You were here, right? And Tanya and Jon, of course, and—"

She broke off. She could hear Alexi calling her name again, from below.

Her blood seemed to chill and congeal. She wanted Alexi to be a murderer, she realized. And yet she had to hear the truth about Dustin.

Geoffrey stared at her kindly as if he understood her dilemma. He winked. "Let's dodge the man, shall we? Come. Let's hurry along."

He took her arm, and she offered him a grateful smile. They rushed along the hallway, passing the telephone niche, then Jon Vadim's room. Carly heard soft words in her sister's voice. She glanced quickly at Geoffrey, but he apparently hadn't noticed.

The real Jon Vadim was in that room, she thought, with her sister. Who was to say that the real Jon was not guilty?

The real Jon had been with Jasmine last night. Unless Jasmine had lied to Carly and herself and Jon Vadim had disappeared beneath the moonlight, just like Dustin Vadim.

It ran in the family. Lunacy ran in the family. That was what Alexi had told her.

And Alexi could have been lying.

"In here," Geoffrey said, opening the door to his room. It was large and overlooked the forest, rather than the courtyard. It was a beautiful view. The draperies were open, and Carly could see all the way down the mountain to the chimneys and spires of the houses and churches in the village.

"How lovely!" she exclaimed.

"Yes, so much beauty, and so much discord."

Carly sobered and turned around. Geoffrey smiled and extended a hand toward two wicker chairs that stood before a table where he had pieces of manuscripts laid out. "I've been working, as you can see. And, of course, I know that you've been working, too. A good way to spend time." He shrugged. "Well, have a seat. Where were we? You were asking me something."

Carly sat down at the table, and he took the second chair. He folded his hands prayer-fashion and grinned a little sadly. "What was it you were asking?"

Carly leaned forward, wetting her lips. "Who else was here? Someone who might have been here now, too."

Geoffrey thought about it for a minute. He shrugged. "No one."

"No one?" A wave of relief rolled over her. Dustin couldn't be the one.... He hadn't been here a year ago, so he couldn't have killed the first girl on that Halloween.

"Are you...sure?"

"Of course. People who are here now were here then. There were Jon and I and Alexi. And Jasmine—she is here now. Tanya," he whispered. "Tanya was here."

"No one else."

"Oh, well, the same as now, no." He frowned pensively for a moment. "Dustin was here last year. But of course, he isn't here now."

"Dustin?" She spoke in barely a whisper. She felt ill. She wondered if Jon had summoned the very demon who had cast suspicion on him.

Dear God, no! If she loved a man so deeply, she had to believe in him.

His slippers had been wet and muddy. He had been gone so long. He had been in the stables, and now...

He had been here last year, as well.

"What's the matter?" Geoffrey inquired quietly.

She shook her head, knowing she was probably white as a sheet.

"Dustin is Jon's cousin. An English fellow. You'll meet him somewhere along the line, I suppose."

"I suppose." She stood up. She had to be alone. "Thanks, Geoffrey."

"Whatever for?"

"The answers...the company."

"Don't worry. They'll let old Jon out soon enough." He laughed. "Then you and Jasmine will have to fight over the poor boy." He sighed. "Tanya, bless her soul, will be out of it."

Carly nodded. She still couldn't believe that Tanya wouldn't waltz in on them with her beautiful feline sway. She shivered, and the truth of it hit her. Tanya was dead. She'd been kind to Carly, and Carly had gotten to know her as a friend. Now she was gone, and so tragically.

"Thanks, Geoffrey," she murmured.

He smiled and waved. She stepped out into the hallway and started toward her own room. As she passed the telephone alcove, Alexi suddenly stepped out to grab her.

"Carly! I've been trying to reach you—"

"Let go of me!" She jerked violently, freeing herself. His lip began to curl into a slow, crooked smile. An evil smile, she thought, sadistic and wicked. "I've been looking for you, trying to talk to you—"

"Leave me alone!"

"But I can show you—"

Carly spun around, backing away from him. "Alexi, I know you went to her again and again. You knew Tanya better than any of us."

"Carly, don't run!"

She kept walking away. She wanted to reach her room. She wanted to slam the door and lock it.

"Carly, I can tell you things."

"I don't want to hear them!"

"I will come after you if you don't listen! I'll break the door down! You have to understand!"

She was suddenly certain that he wanted her to understand what it was that drove him. It was the things that the full, glowing moon could do to the human psyche and to the animal within the human breast....

She was getting hysterical, she told herself. She didn't know what she was doing or where to turn anymore.

She loved Dustin, and yet she just didn't know. He'd been here. So many things suggested that he might be guilty.

"Carly—"

Alexi was staring at her. She clapped her hands over her ears. "No! No! I do not want to hear any more!"

She turned and sped toward her room. She didn't care that he knew that she was running. She entered into her room and slammed the door. She leaned against it, gasping for breath. Moments passed, and her breathing at last began to ease.

"Carly!" It was Alexi. His voice was rasping and sounded funny. He was trying to be very quiet.

"Carly, let me in. I'll break the door down."

She didn't respond. Then she felt the door shudder behind her.

Dustin had already broken the door in once. It would be easy for someone else now.

She stood there in panic and felt it shudder again. In another few seconds the door would burst open and she would be trapped. She had to do something.

She looked across the room to the secret paneling. She was wearing jeans and sneakers and a sweater, and she was ready for a rapid and desperate escape. She was far better dressed for traversing the secret passage now than she had been two weeks ago.

The door shuddered a third time.

Carly didn't wait any longer. She bolted across the room and began to search for the spring button. Panic welled up in her as she heard the door shudder yet again.

"Carly..."

"Please, please, please!..." she prayed. At last she found it, and the panel slid open, allowing her access to the passageway beyond. She slipped in and started down the corridor, just as she heard the door to her room give.

She tried to hurry. The corridor was dark, for the daylight didn't seem to be filtering in at all. What entered was mist. It was eerie and frightening. She could hear her own footfalls and the sound of her breath and the beat of her heart....

Suddenly she stood still. She could hear something else. Someone was behind her. Someone was following her. Alexi?

Alexi...or whoever had whispered to her, whoever had broken into her room.

Following her and moving far more quickly than she was able to move.

She wouldn't be able to get far. She came to the steps that led down and paused, just for a heartbeat.

Someone was coming fast.

She started down the steps, trying to be silent. The light was still dim; the winding stairs were treacherous. She missed her footing and almost fell, and gasped as she clung to the cold stone wall.

She stood still.

And heard whoever was pursuing her pause and listen. She prayed silently.

It was no good. She heard the footsteps behind her coming down the stairs.

She gave a horrified cry, no longer concerned about making noise.

At the landing she came to a dead end—a locked door. Desperate, frantic, she clawed at the bolt.

The steps came after her, then actually slowed and came on at a far more leisurely pace.

"Carly..."

She tugged at the bolt as hard as she could. It creaked and groaned—and gave.

Carly tore outside, into the heavy mist that had fallen. She heard her pursuer swear, and she screamed, rushing forward.

She couldn't see, and didn't know where she was. She could only hope that the man behind her was as blinded by the mist as herself.

She heard a crunch of footsteps on the surface of the courtyard. Coming toward her, homing in unerringly on her position.

"No!" she screamed. He was close, so close she could almost feel him, sense him.

She banged into something. It was a police car, the inspector's car, she realized. He was back.

And that could mean that Dustin was back, that it was Dustin following her, calling her name, relentlessly pursuing her.

"No, please, no!" she whispered again frantically. The car! If she could just get into the car and hide. She tried the door, but it was locked. No one locked a car here. But now, when she was so desperate, the door to the police car was locked, she thought, almost delirious.

The footsteps were still coming. She heard the crunch of the shoes, and it was the stroke of a razor blade down her spine. Closer, closer.

"Help!" she screamed as loudly as she could. She'd given her position away, she knew. She had to move, though she had no idea of where she was or in which direction she should be moving. She screamed again and ran. Something loomed in front of her in the mist. She had reached the stables. Gasping, she inched her way along the wall until she came to the door. She paused, listening, and her heart seemed to cease beating.

Crunch...

She heard it again, the ruthless, merciless sound.

She found the door and wrenched it open. There were lights on here.

They suddenly flickered out, and darkness descended upon her.

"No!" she whispered.

The door jolted closed behind her. Carly ran around, seeking some hiding place. Horses whinnied and snorted, sensing her fear. She hurried along the stalls. She could see nothing, but she could feel the shapes of each stall.

The stable door opened.

Carly lunged into one of the stalls. As silently as she could, she closed the door behind her. She moved around the restless animal and cowered, hunched against the wall, barely daring to breathe.

She heard him. Moving. Walking slowly. Pausing. Walking again.

Then the stall door opened, and a light shone into her face. "Carly..."

A scream rose in her throat. She held up a hand, squinting beyond the light.

It couldn't be! It just couldn't be....

"Yes, Carly. Me..." he said.

She dimly heard the horse whinny and nervously prance out of the way. She didn't have time to move; she barely had time to scream. Then he slammed the flashlight against her head.

They were still in the process of driving back when Dustin first felt the chill of unease. He didn't know what had brought it on, but it seized hold of him like a vise and didn't let go.

"Can't you hurry?" Dustin demanded.

With Gallic abandon the inspector used hand signals to indicate the fog and the impossibility of seeing the road. "I'm going as fast as I can. What is your sudden hurry?"

Dustin gritted his teeth. "Because we know now!"

Irritably LaRue glanced his way again. "We know! We have no proof. Just because this information came in, it doesn't mean we have proof."

"I'm willing to bet my life," Dustin murmured.

"You still owe me one tremendous explanation," LaRue said.

"Yes," Dustin said uncomfortably. LaRue still didn't know who he was. Or if he had guessed, he hadn't let on. And letting him in on the truth still didn't seem a very prudent thing to do. That would leave both Jon and himself vulnerable.

"We're here," Dustin said. The tension was rising in him unbearably. He tried to calm himself, tried to breathe, but couldn't get the fear to subside.

It was Carly. There was no reason why he should be so afraid for her, yet he was. It was daylight; the murderer chose to strike by night. She wouldn't have been alone, anyway. She would have been with Jasmine and Jon, and nobody could touch all three of them, he was certain. And all the servants were there, too, of course.

The inspector had barely parked before Dustin was jumping out of the car. He looked anxiously through the fog. Knowing the layout of the courtyard and the terrace, he made his way through the fog.

"Attendez-moi!" the inspector puffed, breathless. "Count Vadim!"

He couldn't wait. He felt a growing urgency. He paused, thinking he heard a scream.

The inspector crashed into him. "What? What?" LaRue demanded.

He must have imagined it, Dustin thought. He didn't hear anything else. Then he heard a wolf's cry, a high, plaintive cry, as if the creature was confused by the fog.

"Nothing," Dustin muttered. He rushed on into the house. He burst into the library. It was empty.

"God!" he groaned, his sense of urgency mounting.

"Count—" the inspector said at his heels.

"I can't wait!" Dustin snapped. He raced back through the terrace and up the stairs. He burst into Carly's room and saw that she wasn't there. He tried to calm himself. Of course not. She shouldn't be here, alone; she should be with Jon and Jasmine.

He came back into the hallway just as the inspector reached it. He didn't give any explanations; he hurried on toward his cousin's room. He slammed his fist against the door. Jasmine opened it, staring at him anxiously.

"Where's Carly?" he demanded. He stared from Jasmine to Jon. "Oh, God," he said, feeling sick. "She's not with you."

"She's not in her room?" Jasmine demanded.

He shook his head.

The inspector reached them. He looked from Dustin to Jon, then back to Dustin again. "So, I was right. You are back, Dustin Vadim, and you contacted your cronies because of your secret service connections, yes?"

"Yes, but—"

"I ought to arrest you both!"

"Inspector—"

"I will have an explanation, and a long one!" LaRue insisted.

"But not now! Carly is in grave danger. We must find her! Now, before it is too late!" Dustin exclaimed.

Jasmine burst into tears. Dustin stared at Jon, and together they nodded.

"The cottage!" Dustin said. "Where else would he take her?"

"Wait. Maybe she is with Alexi—" Jon began. But at that moment, Alexi came along the corridor, attracted by the noise and the excitement.

Dustin practically picked him up by the lapels. "Alexi, where is Carly? Have you seen her?"

Alexi shook his head. "I tried to talk to her," he said sulkily. "She locked herself in her room."

Dustin dropped him, turned and raced down the stairway. Outside, he blundered his way through the fog. He tore into the stables and found Satan. Satan knew his way through the fog. LaRue and Jon could follow in the car. Dustin couldn't risk a single second.

When Carly awoke, she knew she was near a fire for it was very warm.

Her head ached horribly. She strained to open her eyes, then to lift a hand to her head. But she couldn't move her hand. She realized that she was tied to the bunk and that she was so warm because she was naked and the firelight seemed to be touching her body.

He was bent over the fire. He was wearing a black cape and heating a huge, sharp knife in the flames.

He turned suddenly as if he had sensed that she had awakened. She held back a scream, knowing it could do her no good, and prayed desperately that she could reason with him.

They were in the cottage where Dustin had brought her that first night and where they had spent an entire day making love. She had promised here that she would believe in him. And she had betrayed that promise again and again. She had fallen in love with a man but hadn't given him the faith he deserved. The doubts had torn at her.

Now, ironically, she was here again.

Hysteria bubbled within her again. He was looking at her, and she realized that he was staring at her with eyes that glistened with madness.

"It's almost ready," he told her.

"Geoffrey," she murmured, "you don't want to do this. I'm going to make you costumes. I'm..."

"Beautiful costumes, Carly. You're talented. I enjoy you. I enjoyed the others, too. Carly, it is an honor. I am unique among modern men. Death is so often in vain. Not for you, Carly. You will feed the beast in me. Do you understand?"

He wasn't wearing anything beneath the cape, she realized, though he did have gloves on. That's why he could escape detection so easily, she thought. He would burn the cape and the gloves and wash away any blood. He was good. Ironically, he was sane enough to murder his victims carefully.

Now he was going to kill her. He was going to savagely slit her throat and then he was going to drink her blood. And she was tied to a bunk, and there wasn't a thing that she could do about it.

"No!" she cried frantically. She tugged desperately at the ties that bound her. The rope chafed her wrists, but held tight.

She prayed for reason, for her own sanity. "Geoffrey, you can't do this now. It's all wrong. The moon isn't even up. It's daytime. You'll ruin everything."

He smiled and turned the knife blade in the flame. "It's easier when the blade glows. It slips through flesh as if it was butter. Honestly. It's easy, very easy. The first . . . was messy."

She wondered if she could keep him talking.

For what? she wondered desperately. For how long? Who would learn that she was missing? Who would suspect? . . .

Instinct made her press on, despite her despair. "You mean last Halloween?"

He glanced at her, startled. "Oh, no. The first was years ago. In Brooklyn." A dreamy, faraway light came in his eyes, dark eyes that were glazed by the fire. "It was in Brooklyn. I first felt the full moon touch me, and then I knew that I was one of them. A man among men. A wolf, more powerful. Immortal. I could live forever. The moon was full, and she was in my arms. A little slut of an ingenue. She wanted a part so badly. I gave her one. But it was messy, very messy. I tried to stay away from the theater after that." He paused, frowning. "I think that there was one more. An actress. Or maybe a lighting technician. I don't remember." He gazed back at the blade. "It's ready. It's hot, and it will kiss your throat gently. You will not feel the savage need when I feed."

She was going to throw up.

What would it matter if she was dead?

Carly's tone was reproachful. "Alexi—Alexi was really crazy about Tanya. And you killed her. How could you?" Geoffrey was walking toward her. The blade glittered in the firelight. Perspiration shone on her body. She wanted to start crying, raggedly, desperately. She had to stop him. She had to do something.

"They'll catch you!" she cried.

"No. I am the wolf. I am immortal."

"No! You want them to think that Jon Vadim is the wolf, but they'll know. They'll know that he did not kill me."

He wasn't even listening anymore. He stared at the knife euphorically, then touched her glistening breast. "It will be quick, my beauty. I promise."

No. It could not be happening. Geoffrey Taylor was a respected American artist who had scores of SRO plays to his credit. It could not be happening—but it was.

He smiled at her. "Quick, and gentle..." he whispered.

She saw the silver glitter of his knife, and a scream tore from her throat.

Then the door burst open, and she saw a blur of sudden motion.

Dustin Vadim came into the room like an offensive tackle, slamming into Geoffrey with a force that sent both men flying off their feet. Carly saw the knife raised high; Geoffrey still held it.

"Dustin! Watch the knife!" she screamed. She worked at her bonds with renewed fury. She heard the scuffle and the thud as the two men fought viciously. Then she heard Dustin swearing; she heard every nuance of his proper British accent growing stronger with his rage.

Then she heard a last, crunching blow and everything was silent. And she felt something soft and warm come over her and she looked up.

Up . . . into golden eyes, blazing and fierce and beautifully tender.

"Oh, Dustin . . ." She shivered. He cut her ties.

"Dustin—he killed people in New York."

"I know. When I first began to suspect him, I asked a friend in Manhattan to look into his past. He dug up a few corpses that somehow pointed to Geoffrey Taylor."

"Dustin . . ."

He was cutting her feet free. "What?" he demanded a little curtly.

"Dustin, I'm so sorry. I didn't trust you. I was afraid. Well, you did disappear, and your slippers were wet."

"Damn right you didn't trust me. My slippers were wet just because I was restless and took a walk outside! I heard sounds coming from the stables and checked it out."

She sat up, clasping the blanket around her, rubbing her wrists. "You saved my life."

"Yeah, fine. But I haven't really forgiven you."

"Dustin—"

"Trust is important in a relationship, you know," he observed.

"Dustin."

"What?"

She curled her arms around him and held him close. Her heart was beating atrociously again. She had almost died. She had almost lost all of this and more. She held him tenaciously, as she had held on to life. And she kissed him, with the fire searing them both.

The door burst open a second time. The inspector was there, with Jon and Jasmine and Alexi. The inspector glanced their way briefly, then hurried to Geoffrey where he lay crumpled on the floor. Jasmine began to weep, raced to Carly and Dustin and kissed them both.

"Carly, you're all right! Oh, God!"

Moments passed in pure emotion. Carly held tight to her blanket and kissed them all—even LaRue. She apologized to Alexi, who sheepishly told her that he had just been trying to explain his relationship with Tanya.

"You did love her, Alexi," Carly murmured.

"She didn't love me. But yes, I loved her, and it hurts, and I will miss her, whether she used me or not."

Jon placed a hand on his shoulder. The inspector cleared his throat. "Messieurs Vadim, I will have full explanations on this, and I will have your utmost cooperation."

"Yes, sir, I promise," Dustin said. Jon drew himself up regally, ready with noble disdain. Then Dustin grinned, ignoring them both as he stared at Carly. "Yes, sir, but not just yet. I'm taking Carly out of here."

"In the morning, then," the inspector said gruffly.

"Oh, no, it will have to be later." Dustin's eyes, amber and gold and as warm as the fire, remained fixed on her. He lifted her into his arms, sweeping the modest covering of the blanket along with her. "I'm taking her to Paris tomorrow. And I'm going to marry her as quickly as I can. She's dangerous if you don't keep her under control, you see. I was really worried. If she marries me, she can't testify against me."

"What?" Carly gasped.

Jasmine started to laugh, but Carly barely heard her. Her gaze was fixed on Dustin's as he carried her outside.

Miraculously, the mist was lifting.

"You will marry me, won't you?" he asked.

"Cocky, aren't you? And I never testified against you. Even when I was afraid I defended you," she retorted.

"Oh, yeah, sure!" he scoffed.

"I did!"

"All right. I forgive you."

"You forgive me?"

"Well, I will if you marry me. What do you say?"

Carly pretended to ponder the question, but not for very long. "Yes."

"Yes?"

"Definitely."

He stared down at her tenderly. He was about to kiss her, when Carly gasped suddenly in disbelief.

It was the wolf. The large, silver-gray wolf of her dreams. It was crashing through the trees, through the remaining mist, straight toward them. And just as she had been terrified that the animal meant to consume her that first night, she quivered with fear now, for she had everything in the world to live for.

"Dustin! The wolf—"

The animal charged at him. Dustin swore and lifted Carly higher. "Vixen, damn you, get down!"

"Vixen!" Carly demanded in her turn.

The wolf, as obedient as a puppy, fell at Dustin's feet, rolling and fawning. Carly stared at him. "Vixen?" she repeated.

He shrugged uncomfortably. "Well, she's a pet, you see."

"She's your pet?"

"Jon's pet. Well, all right, we both found her as a pup. We were about fourteen, I guess."

"She's a pet!" Carly was enraged. "You made me think you dared a savage beast and saved my life—and she's a pet?"

"Don't worry. You'll grow to love her." With a grin he started walking toward Satan. Carly slowly started to smile again as he set her upon the magnificent horse. "You owe me a lot of explanations, as well as the inspector!"

He mounted behind her and nuzzled her neck. "We have a lifetime for that," he murmured. "A lifetime."

He nudged Satan in the ribs. The horse took off as if he were flying. Dustin swept her away, safe from the mist.

It could never have happened in Manhattan, she thought. Not this . . .

Magic.

This rough magic. Enchantment, Carly realized, relaxing against him. Enough to last a lifetime. And they would have a lifetime together, she knew. Of learning, exploring . . . explaining.

As soon as they finished with the inspector, of course.

But before that . . . there would be a wedding. And a honeymoon. And more . . .

"Magic," he said aloud.

"Yes," she whispered.

And Satan carried them onward, while a silver wolf ran along beside them.

Epilogue

Midnight.

The witching hour.

The French doors to the patio were open, and Carly could see the moon high over the black velvet of the night.

The full moon...

The breeze lifted the white draperies and sent them softly floating about, pale and ethereal against the panoply of the night sky. A stronger gust of wind came now and then and cast them about more strenuously. But Carly did not move to close the doors. She welcomed the breeze as she welcomed the night.

She longed to welcome her lover.

She was dressed in white herself. Soft, shimmering white that hung in silken folds about her body. Her shoulders were bare except for two slim straps that held the low-cut bodice of the nightgown to her breasts. Shadows fell against the creamy mounds so displayed by the gown and darkened the valley between them. Soft, sheer gauze flowed from the tight bodice to the floor and hauntingly displayed the shape and substance of the woman beneath.

She was obviously a woman awaiting a lover.

Suddenly she cried out. He was there, coming to her from out of the darkness. Forgetting what she was wearing, she raced out to meet him, throwing her arms around him.

"Dustin! What happened? Did he understand? He isn't still angry, is he? I mean, LaRue must understand by now that you had to do what you did!"

Dustin laughed and easily swung her off her feet. Carly rested her hands on his shoulders and stared down into his eyes. "Dustin, please, tell me. Is everything all right?"

"Yes, everything is fine."

"Oh!" she said simply.

Suddenly they heard a whistle. A wolf whistle that came from nearby.

"Let's get in, shall we?" Dustin suggested. He lowered her against the length of him, grinning. He caught her hand, and they hurried inside together. Let the young ones prowl, he thought. Let them whistle and envy him his mate.

They entered the room, and Dustin carefully closed and locked the door behind him. He swept Carly up and over to the bed, grinning as they lay down together. He tried to kiss her, but she pressed against him.

"Dustin!"

He sighed. "Oh, all right. LaRue knows he can't really arrest either of us—if it hadn't been for my friend in Manhattan who did the research on Geoffrey, we might never have caught up with him. You know

LaRue. He did hem and haw about my being in the country illegally. But then, Jon is nobility, and it isn't wise for LaRue to get on his bad side. He's a socially conscious man, you know."

Carly nodded and smiled. She did know LaRue. Her smile faded. "What about Geoffrey? Are they going to... hang him?"

Dustin shook his head. "Geoffrey is terribly ill. He'll be confined for life. He'll never leave the hospital."

"Thank God," Carly breathed.

He kissed her, as if the warmth of his kiss could forever dispel the threat of the grave. "They're getting married next month."

"No!" Carly pushed him away. "Jon and Jasmine? Really! How wonderful!"

"It will be the social event of the season."

Carly laughed. "Yes, knowing Jasmine, I think it will be."

Dustin hesitated a minute. "You really don't mind, do you? I mean... Well, you did fall in love with a count. We ran away and got married in a little church on a corner in Paris. The count comes with a castle, but I'm afraid *you'll* be getting a Tudor house in Surrey."

She offered him a dazzling smile that touched her turquoise eyes. She played her fingers through his hair and watched him with humor and fascination.

"First of all, I thought our wedding was wonderfully romantic. I think that 'mister' is a grand title. And I really think that the castle will always give me a few chills, while I absolutely adore London. We'll be keeping my apartment in Manhattan, too. But then most of all..."

"Most of all what?" he inquired. He lowered his head, and the tip of his tongue teased her throat.

"Most of all, I am just exquisitely in love with the man, the wolf I met in the woods."

"You've got to be very careful of wolves in the woods," he warned her.

As if on cue, they heard a chorus of wolves howling, crying to the full moon.

Carly laughed delightedly. "Your comrades are out there," she said lightly.

"Well, darling, this wolf doesn't need to howl to the moon any longer."

"No?"

"He's found everything that he could ever ask, right here in your arms."

"Oh, Dustin, that's so lovely."

"Thank you," he told her.

Then she saw the color change in his eyes, from amber to a heated, glowing gold. She knew the signs, knew the language of his body.

And when he kissed her she felt his ardor, swift and sure and certain.

The wolves continued to howl their curious serenade. But Carly scarcely heard them anymore, for the flame of her love seemed to crackle and heat and the beasts held no threat for her, for she was secure in the love of her one particular, passionate, stormy, stubborn, somewhat arrogant and still beautiful wolf. She knew now that neither of them would ever stray from the other. Love had struck too deeply. It had come like magic, against all odds, against fear and danger, and it would remain—magic.

"Grrr..." he murmured, growling his content.

She laughed until the quickening flames rendered her incapable of any more laughter, and she cried out her love instead.

* * * * *

TALES OF THE RISING MOON
A Desire trilogy by Joyce Thies

MOON OF THE RAVEN—June (#432)

Conlan Fox was part American Indian and as tough as the Montana land he rode, but it took fragile yet strong-willed Kerry Armstrong to make his dreams come true.

REACH FOR THE MOON—August (#444)

It would take a heart of stone for Steven Armstrong to evict the woman and children living on his land. But when Steven saw Samantha, eviction was the last thing on his mind!

GYPSY MOON—October (#456)

Robert Armstrong met Serena when he returned to his ancestral estate in Connecticut. Their fiery temperaments clashed from the start, but despite himself, Rob was falling under the Gypsy's spell.

SD 456

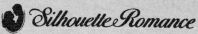
Silhouette Romance

LONG, TALL TEXANS

A Trilogy by Diana Palmer

Bestselling Diana Palmer has rustled up three rugged heroes in a trilogy sure to lasso your heart! The titles of the books are your introduction to these unforgettable men:

CALHOUN

In June, you met Calhoun Ballenger. He wanted to protect Abby Clark from the world, but could he protect her from himself?

JUSTIN

In August, Calhoun's brother, Justin—the strong, silent type—had a second chance with the woman of his dreams, Shelby Jacobs.

TYLER

October's long, tall Texan is Shelby's virile brother, Tyler, who teaches shy Nell Regan to trust her instincts—especially when they lead her into his arms!

Don't miss TYLER, the last of three gripping stories from Silhouette Romance!

Silhouette Intimate Moments

COMING
NEXT MONTH

#261 SMOKE SCREEN—Emilie Richards

Paige Duvall had come to Waimauri, New Zealand, to forget a painful past, not embark upon a future. But then she met handsome sheep farmer Adam Tomoana, a man who held the secret to her heritage, and quite possibly her heart.

#262 FLOWER OF THE DESERT—Barbara Faith

Strong-willed Princeton coed Jasmine Hasir had always been able to take care of herself. But that was before she was kidnapped by a nomadic horseman in the lawless Sahara sands. Then only the power of love—and Raj Hajad—would be able to rescue her.

#263 CROSSCURRENTS—Linda Turner

Mitch Flannery had never trusted anyone; his work in the Secret Service had taught him that. But his prime suspect, Serenity Jones, had too much integrity to be a criminal. And when she became a killer's prime target, Mitch had to learn a new lesson. Only his faith could give them a future—together.

#264 THE NAME OF THE GAME—Nora Roberts

Television game show producer Johanna Patterson knew the larger-than-life people of show business were just that: unreal. But she soon realized that actor/contestant Sam Weaver wasn't playing a game. He *really* was determined to gain her trust—and win her love.

AVAILABLE THIS MONTH:

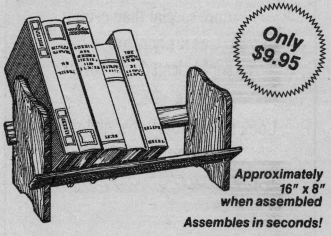

In October
Silhouette Special Edition
becomes
more special than ever
as it premieres
its sophisticated new cover!

Look for six soul-satisfying novels
every month...from
Silhouette Special Edition

SERLB-1